P9-CMN-451

Bunnicula Meets
Meets
Edgar Allan Crow

BOOKS BY
JAMES HOWE

Bunnicula Books
Bunnicula
  (with Deborah Howe)
Howliday Inn
The Celery Stalks at
  Midnight
Nighty-Nightmare
Return to Howliday Inn
Bunnicula Strikes Again!

Bunnicula and
  Friends
The Vampire Bunny
Hot Fudge
Scared Silly
Rabbit-cadabra!
The Fright Before Christmas

Picture Books
There's a Monster Under
  My Bed
There's a Dragon in My
  Sleeping Bag
Teddy Bear's Scrapbook
  (with Deborah Howe)
Horace and Morris but
  Mostly Dolores
Horace and Morris Join
  the Chorus (but what
  about Dolores?)
Kaddish for Grandpa in
  Jesus' name amen

Tales from the
  House of Bunnicula
It Came from Beneath
  the Bed!
Invasion of the Mind
  Swappers from
  Asteroid 6!
Howie Monroe and the
  Doghouse of Doom
Screaming Mummies of
  the Pharaoh's Tomb II
Bud Barkin, Private Eye
The ~~Amazing~~ Odorous
  Adventures of Stinky Dog

Sebastian Barth
  Mysteries
What Eric Knew
Stage Fright
Eat Your Poison, Dear
Dew Drop Dead

Pinky and Rex Series
Pinky and Rex
*Pinky and Rex Get
  Married*
*Pinky and Rex and the
  Mean Old Witch*
*Pinky and Rex and the
  Spelling Bee*
*Pinky and Rex Go to
  Camp*
*Pinky and Rex and the
  New Baby*
*Pinky and Rex and the
  Double-Dad Weekend*
*Pinky and Rex and the
  Bully*
*Pinky and Rex and the
  New Neighbors*
*Pinky and Rex and the
  Perfect Pumpkin*
*Pinky and Rex and the
  School Play*
*Pinky and Rex and the
  Just-Right Pet*

Novels
A Night Without Stars
Morgan's Zoo
The Watcher
The Misfits
Totally Joe

**Edited by
  James Howe**
*The Color of Absence:
  Twelve Stories about
  Loss and Hope*
*13: Thirteen Stories
  That Capture the Agony
  and Ecstasy of Being
  Thirteen*

Bunnicula Meets Edgar Allan Crow

by JAMES HOWE

ILLUSTRATED BY ERIC FORTUNE

ALADDIN PAPERBACKS
New York London Toronto Sydney

ALADDIN PAPERBACKS
An imprint of Simon & Schuster Children's Publishing Division
1230 Avenue of the Americas, New York, NY 10020
Text copyright © 2006 by James Howe
Illustrations copyright © 2006 by Eric Fortune
All rights reserved, including the right of reproduction in whole or in part in any form.
ALADDIN PAPERBACKS and related logo are
registered trademarks of Simon & Schuster, Inc.
Also available in an Atheneum Books for Young Readers hardcover edition.
The text of this book was set in Stempl Garamond.
The illustrations were rendered in graphite pencil.
Manufactured in the United States of America
First Aladdin Paperbacks edition August 2008
2 4 6 8 10 9 7 5 3 1
The Library of Congress has cataloged the hardcover edition as follows:
Howe, James, 1946–
Bunnicula meets Edgar Allan Crow / James Howe ; illustrated by Eric Fortune. —1st ed.
p. cm.
"Ginee Seo Books"
Summary: An overly alarmed Chester the cat predicts a gruesome fate for the pets
in the Monroe household when a writer of juvenile horror fiction and his bird
companion stay overnight.
ISBN-13: 978-1-4169-1458-7 (hc.)
ISBN-10: 1-4169-1458-7 (hc.)
[1. Pets—Fiction. 2. Authors—Fiction. 3. Crows—Fiction. 4. Humorous stories.]
I. Fortune, Eric, ill. II. Title
PZ7.H83727Bum 2006
[Fic]—dc22 2006000574
ISBN-13: 978-1-4169-1473-0 (pbk.)
ISBN-10: 1-4169-1473-0 (pbk.)

TO MEREDITH AND WILL DAVIS

—J. H.

CONTENTS

It was with a heavy heart that I entered my office that Friday afternoon in December. After the holidays, I would be cleaning out my desk one last time—not because my publishing house was moving to a new office but because I was moving to a new life. I wanted to believe that I'd made the right decision. After all, I'd yearned to take up sheep farming for as long as I could remember. Still, when I opened that door and beheld the shelves overflowing with books; the framed photos, plaques, and awards covering the walls; the sharpened pencils with their worn-down erasers; and the half-read manuscripts and half-eaten candy bars littering my desk, I couldn't help asking: Could sheep bring me anywhere near the pleasure I'd found in the company of authors?

As I sank into my Dusty Mauve Naugahyde Chair Ergonomically Sculpted with Lumbar Support Curvature—a bonus I'd received as part of a recent job promotion—I felt myself sink into a dusty melancholia as well. I picked up a copy of the latest self-help bestseller written by one of my authors, *Dr. Bob's Grab Yourself Some Happiness, Even If It Makes You Miserable*, and flipped to a random page, hoping to find reassurance that I was doing the right thing.

Finding nothing on that page or any other to offer me answers (I began to wonder how the book had ever made it onto the bestseller lists, but felt it best not to pursue that line of thinking), I reached instead for the handle of the top right-hand drawer of my desk. I hesitated. What I kept in that drawer was there only "in case of emergency."

Slowly I pulled the drawer open. I couldn't find what I was looking for at first. I'd carefully hidden it from the eyes of my assistant, a former circus clown who liked to sneak into my office on weekends to reorganize my files and leave little balloon animals on my desk as a Monday morning surprise. But then my fingers touched it. I pulled the desired object out from under a legal pad and asked myself if I really wanted to do something so drastic. I had just come from the office holiday party, after all. I was full of eggnog and seven-layer cake. But the rich aroma of dark chocolate was too much to resist. I loosened my belt a notch and slid the bar from its wrapper, peeled back the foil, and was about to take my first bite when I was overcome by despondency.

To eat chocolate . . . alone . . . behind a closed door . . . had it come to this?

I let my gaze drift to the door, my mind a whirlwind of chocolate and sheep and balloon animals, when suddenly I heard a familiar scratching. Could it be? Was it possible? After all these years and with no thought that he would write another book?

I bolted to the door, yanked it open, and beheld him: a sad-eyed, droopy-eared dog carrying a large, plain envelope in his mouth. I nearly wept for joy. Harold! Here to save me from eating chocolate alone! Here to present me his latest manuscript, and with it my opportunity to go out in glory! I could think of no way I would rather end my publishing career than editing one of Harold's books.

I broke off a piece of chocolate, offered it to the canine author, and sat down to read the letter clipped to the top page of the manuscript.

My dear friend,

With the publication of my previous book, I had thought my writing career was at its end. But while a writer's career may end, a writer's life goes on. How does one close one's mind to experiences that practically cry out to be recorded? And once recorded, how does one resist the temptation to share them with others?

Once again the events of my life were transformed from the mundane to the mysterious by strange circumstances—and even stranger strangers. I hastened to write them down, the result being the manuscript you now hold in your hands. I know that my books can only aspire to the bestseller status of Dr. Bob's, but I hope that you will find my words worthy of publication nonetheless. They may be the last to find their way into print, for though I say I "hastened" to write them down, the pace of the writing itself was painfully slow. Arthritis has worked its way into these old paws of mine, and the words themselves don't come as quickly as they once did.

Still, I felt compelled to tell this tale of writers and writing, of muses and the bemused, of crows and creativity. Oh, and did I mention terror? There is terror in this tale as well. It is, after all, about a bird named Edgar Allan Crow.

Yours sincerely,
Harold X.

I felt my pulse quicken as I reached for my trusty No. 2 pencil and turned to the first page of Harold's book. Little did I know that his words would do far more than entertain me. For here, in these pages that you yourself, dear reader, are about to enter, I would find the answers I had been seeking.

Bunnicula Meets
Edgar Allan Crow

ONE

The Letter

The trouble began with a letter that arrived at three o'clock on an early October afternoon. The hour was struck by the grandfather clock not far from where I lay dozing near the front door of the house. Howie began yipping his puppy head off at the unseen mailman on the other side of the door, and before I could think to move, a cascade of paper came showering down on me from the mail slot over my head. All in all, it was an ominous awakening.

"Howie," I said, shaking off my drowsiness along with the envelopes and magazines, "that's Joe. He's not here to rob us; he's here to deliver the mail. You know Joe. Why do you always bark at him?"

Howie looked appalled that I would ask such a question. "It's my job," he declared, "my duty as a canine. Gee, Uncle Harold." (Howie calls me Uncle Harold even though we're not related. I guess it's because he looks up to me—and who can blame him for that?)

Chester jumped down from his favorite chair in the adjoining room and sauntered over. "And you call yourself a dog," he snickered.

"I am a dog," I replied defensively. "I just don't care for the sound of barking. You know that, Chester."

Chester didn't respond. Distracted by something he'd spotted in the pile of scattered pieces of mail, he let out a loud gasp.

"What is it?" I asked, the hairs rising along the ridge of my back. If I hadn't been half-asleep, I might have had the good sense to keep that particular question to myself, knowing as I do that Chester's gasping is rarely cause for alarm. He is, after all, a cat, which means he tends toward the, shall we say, dramatic.

"Look for yourself!" he went on, jabbing a paw at the envelope lying closest to me. "It's a crow!"

"Did you say 'crow'?" Howie asked excitedly. He darted down the hall, through the kitchen, and out the pet door before you could call out, "Be back in time for dinner!"

Chester shook his head. "I fail to understand Howie's obsession with chasing birds," he said.

I sighed. "It must be part of his job."

"Well," said Chester, "one of these days his 'job' is going to get him into a heap of trouble. Crows are not to be messed with, my friend. They're nefarious. Just look at that one."

Yawning, I glanced at the crow on the envelope to see what all the fuss was about. What I saw was a crow. On an envelope. I didn't think it looked particularly nefarious. Of course, I had no idea what "nefarious" meant. When I asked Chester for a definition, he started bathing his tail.

"Aha!" I said. "You're stalling. You don't know what 'nefarious' means either, Mr. Big Words Fancy Pants!"

Ordinarily, Chester would have been offended by being called Mr. Big Words Fancy Pants, but apparently he didn't care to be offended. He also didn't care to define "nefarious."

"I'll tell you this," he went on, dropping his tail. I noticed there was a hair stuck to his tongue. "Crows are omens, Harold."

I rolled my eyes. Chester sees omens everywhere. Just the other day, he thought he saw an omen in Mr. Monroe's oatmeal. I pointed out that it was a raisin.

"Raisins can't be omens?" he'd asked.

I would love to tell you that Chester is a deep thinker, but I don't think "deep" is quite the right word. I, however, have been known to think deeply on occasion. And that is what I was doing now as I studied the image of the crow on the envelope. It looked familiar somehow.

Just then a key turned in the door. Having a pretty good idea of who would be coming in, I leaped to my feet to get out of the way fast. Pete, the older of the two boys with whom I reside, burst into the house, his flying backpack preceding him. The backpack landed with a thud and slid down the hall toward the kitchen, sending Chester scampering halfway up the stairs to the second floor.

"What's the matter with *him*?" Chester hissed. "He's even grumpier than usual."

As if Pete actually understood what Chester was saying (which he never does; unlike his younger brother, Toby, Pete is as thick as Alpo when it comes to understanding us pets), he stomped into the living room, kicked the corner of the sofa, and snarled,

"I'm never speaking to Kyle again!" It was a good thing Mrs. Monroe wasn't there. She doesn't approve of kicking sofas. (She doesn't approve of chewing pillows, either. But that's another story.)

Now, I'm not what you'd call Pete's biggest fan. Toby I can't get enough of, but Pete? Let me put it this way. Ever since he was five and decided I'd look better with what he called a "military cut," I've tried to steer clear of the kid. It's been seven years and I'm still not convinced that all my hair has grown back. Still, I couldn't help but feel sorry for him. Kyle has been his best friend from even before the unfortunate haircutting incident. They'd had fights before. Friends fight. Why, even Chester and I have been known to have our little disagreements from time to time. But I'd never seen Pete kick a sofa because of Kyle. This was serious.

I decided the best strategy was to give my attention to Toby, who was just coming in the door. I greeted him with my usual enthusiasm, which is to say heavy whimpering, a few deep-throated woofs, lots of licks, and what we in the dog trade call the "I'm-your-best-friend-so-please-please-please-don't-ever-leave-me-again" treatment. Toby bent down and let me lick his face all over, then patted me on the head. He tried to pat Chester's head, too, but Chester would have none of it. He pulled away, demonstrating what those in the cat trade call the "If-you-think-you-can-make-up-for-leaving-me-by-giving-me-a-lousy-pat-on-the-head-when-you-get-back-you'd-better-think-again-Buster" treatment.

Toby grabbed his brother by his arm and said, "Hey, thanks a lot for waiting up for me!"

"I was in a hurry, okay? It's not my problem if you can't keep up!" Pete said, yanking his arm away so hard he almost toppled over. How Toby and Pete have arrived at the ages of ten and twelve without losing body parts I have no idea.

Before Toby could say anything else, Pete's pocket rang. Okay, it wasn't really his pocket. It was this thing *in* his pocket called a cell phone. He'd been given it as a birthday present a few weeks earlier. Why a twelve-year-old boy needs to carry a phone in his pocket is beyond me. All I can say is, it's only a matter of time until Chester has a cell phone (even if he doesn't have a pocket), and when he does: Watch out!

Pete pulled the phone out of his pocket, flipped it open, and yelled, "I'm not talking to you!"

People are so amusing. I mean, to tell the person

you're talking to that you're not talking to them? You have to admit, it's pretty funny.

Anyway, the next thing Pete said to whoever it was he wasn't talking to was, "Oh, yeah?" (Pete says, "Oh, yeah?" a lot.) "Well, who cares if you think M. T. Graves isn't a real person? He *is* real and he *is* cool and I don't care if you and everybody in the whole school or the whole world or the whole *universe* thinks his books are so over! They are so *not*—and you know it! They're awesome! And I wrote to him and told him so. So there!"

Pete snapped his cell phone shut and glared at his little brother, who was staring at him.

"You wrote to M. T. Graves?" Toby asked.

"Yes, I wrote to M. T. Graves. Want to make something of it?"

Toby shook his head. "No, I think it's cool. I mean, I like the FleshCrawlers books, too."

That was it! The crow on the envelope was the same as the one on the covers of the FleshCrawlers books. I knew about the FleshCrawlers series because not only did Pete read them all the time, they were Howie's favorite books as well. Howie read them over Pete's shoulder and had them all practically memorized. Maybe the picture of the crow on the envelope meant that the letter was from M. T. Graves! I grabbed it with my teeth and trotted over to Pete.

"Get away from me!" he shouted when he saw me coming. Do you begin to grasp why Pete is not my absolute, number one favorite person in the world? "And what are you doing with that letter? Are you going to eat it? Harold, that is so gross!"

I dropped the envelope at his feet and whimpered.

"Do you want to go for a walk?" said Pete. "Toby, it's your turn to walk Harold and Howie."

Correction: Pete Monroe is even *thicker* than Alpo.

"He probably wants his snack," Toby said. "I'll get it in a minute. So how come you wrote to M. T. Graves? What did you say?"

"It was an assignment for school. We had to write to an author. Everybody else chose J. K. Rowling or James Howe, but I picked M. T. Graves. And not just because he writes the best books."

Toby nodded his agreement.

"I also wrote him because his publisher was having this contest called 'Why FleshCrawlers Gross Me Out the Most.' I entered the contest with my letter. That's called killing two birds with one stone. No offense to Edgar Allan Crow."

"Who?" Toby asked.

"Duh. Edgar Allan Crow. *Everybody* knows that's the name of his pet crow. You know, the one on the books. The FleshCrawlers logo! See?"

Pete ran to his backpack, dug through it, and yanked out a copy of *The House That Dripped Eyeballs* (FleshCrawlers #61). Reading from the back cover, he said, "'M. T. Graves lives in a creepy castle on a remote mountaintop with only his bats, snakes, alligators, and favorite pet Edgar Allan Crow for companionship.'"

No dogs? I thought as I picked up the envelope again and whimpered even louder.

Toby looked over at me. I looked into his eyes. I said with my eyes, *Take this envelope out of my mouth. Look at it. Read the letter inside.*

"I think Harold's trying to tell us something," Toby said.

Pete = Alpo. Toby = genius.

Toby removed the envelope from my mouth. "Look at this!" he cried. "It's Edgar Allan Crow!"

At that moment Howie came racing in, breathless with excitement. "Did I just hear 'Edgar Allan Crow'?" he asked, panting rapidly.

"Yes," I told him, in as calming a voice as I could manage. "Pete wrote to M. T. Graves and—"

"Pete wrote to M. T. *Graves*?"

"Yes, Howie, Pete wrote to M. T. Graves, and M. T. Graves wrote back, and—"

"M. T. Graves wrote *back*?"

"Yes, Howie, and that envelope—"

"And that *envelope*?"

"Howie!" Chester snapped from the stairs. "You'll give me a migraine."

"Okay, Pop," Howie said, "I will just as soon as I can find one. But first I want to hear about—"

"M. T. Graves!" Pete shouted, his hands shaking as he held the open letter out in front of him.

"So it *is* from him!" said Toby.

"Not only that," said Pete. "It says I won the contest! I can't believe it! M. T. Graves is coming to visit our school! And get this: He's going to stay at our house!"

Howie began to howl.

"And he's bringing Edgar Allan Crow!"

Chester began to hiss.

Toby and Pete looked at them. "We really do have very weird pets," Pete said.

He grabbed his backpack and raced Toby up the stairs, nearly knocking Chester over in the process.

"I can't wait to tell Mom and Dad!" I heard Pete

shout. "But first I'm going to call Kyle and tell him that M. T. Graves is real! Ha!" Pete's door slammed shut.

Chester's eyes met mine. "The crow is coming," he murmured. "The crow is coming, Harold. Do you know what that means?"

"Um, it means . . . we'll be having corn for dinner?"

"No, Harold. It does not mean we'll be having corn for dinner. It means we're doomed. That's what it means."

"Oh," I said. "Well, that's a relief. Corn gets stuck in my teeth."

TWO

Excellently Weird

That night at dinner Mr. and Mrs. Monroe couldn't stop talking about their brilliant son. I don't mean Toby, the really brilliant one. I mean Pete, the temporarily brilliant one.

"We didn't even know you'd entered this contest, Pete," Mr. Monroe was saying as he sat down at the table and I was moving into my usual spot next to Toby's chair. Toby has been known to slip me a little something from time to time when nobody's looking. Like I said: The kid's brilliant.

"I didn't want anyone to know about it," Pete answered. "In case I lost."

"Oh, Pete," said Mrs. Monroe, "we wouldn't

have thought anything of it if you had lost. I just can't believe you *won*—out of so many entries! I want to read that letter again."

Mrs. Monroe passed by me on her way to her seat, carrying a platter of meat loaf in one hand and the letter from M. T. Graves in the other. After a silent, unanswered prayer that the meat loaf platter might slip from her fingers, I listened as she pulled her chair out and began to read the letter aloud.

> *Dear Peter Monroe,*
>
> *Congratulations! After personally reading all fifteen thousand entries in the "Why Flesh-Crawlers Gross Me Out the Most" contest, I have selected yours as the winner! I am delighted that my books gross you out so much, but what impressed me even more was what you wrote about yourself and your family. I particularly enjoyed your description of your unusual pets.*
>
> *As you know, the winner of this contest receives a visit by me to his or her school. I look forward to visiting your school, Peter! My publisher will be in contact with you about the details. Ordinarily, I would ask to be put up in a hotel, but you have made your family—especially your pets—sound so intriguing*

*that I wonder if I might be so bold as to ask for lodg-
ing in your home. I will be bringing my good friend
Edgar Allan Crow with me. Please be sure to ask
your parents if they would very much mind housing
an author and his corvine companion.*

*Until we meet, and with my gratitude for
your enthusiastic support of my work, I am*

Yours truly,
M. T. Graves

*P.S. I'm looking forward to spending some
quality time with your special pets!*

"What do you think?" I asked Chester. As was
his habit during meals, he was curled up under the
table. Howie was curled up next to him.

"What do I think?" Chester said. "The guy read
fifteen thousand entries on why his books are gross.
He needs a life, that's what I think."

"Maybe that explains it," Howie remarked.
"Maybe M. T. Graves has been so busy reading all
those contest entries he hasn't had time to write any
books. There haven't been any new ones in a long
time. Pete and I have been worried."

Just then Mr. Monroe asked, "Pete, would you reread that part of your letter where you wrote about the animals? It was so descriptive."

I could hear Pete's big sigh even from under the table. "If I *have* to," he said.

"Ooh, poor Pete," Toby moaned. "Has to read his prize-winning letter *again*. Too bad I didn't even know there *was* a contest!"

"Jealous!"

"Am not!"

"Are too!"

"Boys!" Mrs. Monroe interjected in a no-nonsense tone.

"Fine," Pete said. I heard him rustling some papers, and then:

"'And the number one reason I think your books are the grossest is the excellently weird animals you put in them. I have pets who are weird, too, although they are not always excellently so.'"

Hmm. Do I bite him now or later?

"'I have two dogs. Harold is big and old. He drools a lot.'"

Now.

"'My brother Toby gives Harold chocolate treats, which everybody knows you're not supposed to do, because chocolate can make dogs sick. I don't think it has hurt Harold, though, except maybe in the brains department. He's no Einstein, if you know what I mean.'"

Okay, so I wouldn't really bite Pete. I'm not a biter. But I was considering some serious drooling on his foot when a piece of meat loaf suddenly materialized before me. I gratefully accepted it from Toby's fingers. When I looked up to say thanks, I found him looking down at me with a worried expression on his face. I knew what he was thinking. Pete had given away our secret! Now that Mr. and Mrs. Monroe knew, would there be no more treats for my sweet tooth? How would I live without the occasional chocolate cupcake with cream in the center? Luckily, Mr. and Mrs. Monroe didn't seem to be paying attention to anything other than Pete's literary genius. Personally, I couldn't help wondering how Mr. Monroe, who is a college professor of literature, could be proud of anyone who wrote "excellently weird." But for the moment at least, it looked like my future relationship with chocolate was secure.

Pete read on:

"'Then there's Howie. He's this wirehaired

dachshund puppy we got at this boarding kennel called Chateau Bow-Wow. He chases birds and barks at cars, and sometimes he lets out these totally bizarre howls that could make your flesh crawl. (Get it?) You'd probably like it when he howls, though. You'd think he was possessed or something. I mean, really, he could be a character in one of your books.'"

Poor Howie, I thought—until I noticed the dreamy smile on his face.

"Wow." He sighed. "A character in an M. T. Graves novel. How awesome would *that* be?"

Chester shuddered. "Oh, yeah, right," he said, "that's what *I* live for—to be a psycho-creature in one of M. T. Graves's demented novels. Is this guy totally warped or something? What's he got against reality?"

Pete continued:

"'But wait, it gets even weirder. Chester is our cat. But he's not what you'd call a *normal* cat. He's more like a cat from outer space. Sometimes he gets this look in his eyes like he's beaming in messages from the home planet. And sometimes he does stuff that you'd have to be from a whole other galaxy to even *think* about doing! Like one time we came home and found him pounding a sirloin steak on top of our sound-asleep rabbit! Is he unreal or what?'"

Chester lifted his chin and said, "Reality is so overrated."

"Hey, I wonder what Pete will say about Bunnicula," Howie said.

I don't know if I'd describe our bunny as "excellently weird," but he is definitely unusual. Chester is convinced that Bunnicula is a vampire just because he's turned a few vegetables white by draining them of their juices. Oh, and he can get in and out of his cage without anyone knowing how he does it. And he sleeps all day and is awake at night. And he has these fangs, and . . . well, Pete was doing a pretty good job of describing him, so I'll let him take it from here:

"'If you think Chester's weird, you haven't heard anything yet. We have this rabbit called Bunnicula. We named him that after we found him at a movie theater where *Dracula* was playing. When he came to live with us, our vegetables starting turning white. It took us a while to figure out that maybe he had something to do with it. Ever since we did, he's been on a liquid diet, and there have been no more white vegetables. Other than the vegetable thing, he's not so bad. I mean, he doesn't drool or howl or beam in messages from his home planet or anything. In fact, you might even say he's kind of cute and cuddly. Of course, he does have these red eyes that glow in the dark.

"'In conclusion, Mr. M. T. Graves: You might *write* some weird stuff, but with pets like mine, I *live* it!'"

Mr. and Mrs. Monroe couldn't help breaking into applause. I, meanwhile, couldn't help wolfing down the piece of broccoli Toby had just lowered to me.

Chester shook his head. "Broccoli! You aren't just weird, Harold. You're *excellently* weird."

"Why, thank you, Chester," I said, my tongue trying to nab some florets that had strayed to my whiskers. "It's nice to be appreciated."

"Yes, well, appreciate *this*, my excellently weird friend. There's something mighty peculiar going on here—and I'm not talking about broccoli. I'm talking about M. T. Graves and his 'corvine companion.' Meet me in the living room after the others have gone to sleep and I've had a chance to do some research."

"May I come too, Pop?" Howie asked.

Chester rolled his eyes at being called Pop. It's an automatic response at this point, since Howie has called Chester "Pop" for as long as he's been calling me "Uncle Harold."

"Yes, yes, you may come, too," he said.

And so it was that a little before midnight Howie and I found ourselves stationed in front of Chester's favorite chair in the living room. Sitting amid stacks of FleshCrawlers books, Chester looked down at us and warned, "There is trouble ahead. I told you that crow was an omen."

"What are you talking about?" I asked, stifling a yawn.

"*The Potato Has a Thousand Eyes, My Sister the Pickled Brain, My Parents Are Aliens from the Planet Zorg, Don't Eat the Cookies!*—that's what I'm talking about, Harold."

"Chester," I said, "do you remember when you went to see that nice psychiatrist, Dr. Katz? Do you remember how much he helped you?"

"I do not need a psychiatrist, Harold!"

"Okay, then, do you remember when you used to meditate? Do you remember how it calmed you down and helped you think clearly? Shall we try that now? Shall we chant? Help me out here, Howie. *Om. Ommmm.*"

Chester's eyes narrowed to slits. "I do not need to

meditate and I do not need therapy. What I'm trying to tell you—"

"I know what you're trying to tell us, Pop," Howie chimed in. "Those are the names of FleshCrawlers books. You're trying to tell us . . . um, you're trying to tell us . . . um, names of FleshCrawlers books?"

"Listen to this," Chester said, pushing open the pages of one of the books on the chair.

"Belinda! Belinda, come back!" Tiffani-Sue called out. "You mustn't go into that flying saucer! If you do, you will be turned into a robot!" But it was too late for Belinda, Tiffani-Sue's beloved miniature poodle, the miniature poodle she had been given on her sixth birthday when her mother had been away on yet another of her many business trips, the miniature poodle that had been her best friend and companion ever since her father swam off with his scuba-diving instructor, never to return, when Tiffani-Sue was in the second grade. Now she watched in horror as Belinda was transformed into a steel-plated robot right before her very eyes! "No!" she cried out. "Not you, too, Belinda!"

Howie was blinking back tears. "I wish I could write like that," he said with a sigh.

"And what about this?" Chester went on, pushing open the pages of a different book.

Sara-Ellen Lafferty felt something moving at the bottom of her bed. At first she was scared, but then she remembered that it was only her pet kitten, Mister Buttons. "Whew," Sara-Ellen said to Mister Buttons, "for a moment there I thought you were one of them."

"Who says I'm not?" Mister Buttons replied in an unfamiliar, husky voice.

Sara-Ellen reached for the flashlight her mother had left by her bed just in case she had another of those terrible nightmares. She switched it on. What she beheld made her wish that she was dreaming. But this was real—and more terrible than any nightmare Sara-Ellen had ever had. Now she watched in horror as Mister Buttons was transformed into a steel-plated demon right before her very eyes! "No!" she cried out. "Not you, too, Mister Buttons!"

"And so it goes," said Chester. "In every book, the main character's pet is transformed into something unspeakable!"

"Not to mention steel-plated," I commented.

"If it's unspeakable, then why speak of it?" Howie asked.

"Because it could happen to *us*, don't you see? These so-called novels of his may be no more than thinly disguised blueprints for the horrors he actually commits!" Chester was getting more excited with each word. "Why is he staying in our house? He's a famous author. He should be staying in a hotel, but no, he says he wants to stay here because he wants to meet the pets! He even asks for 'quality time' with us. What is *that* supposed to mean? I'll tell you what it means. It means 'transformation time,' that's what it means!"

"Now, Chester," I said. "I think you're getting a little carried—"

"You want proof, Harold? Is that what you want?"

"I'd rather have a sandwich," I told him. I'm always a little peckish around midnight.

Chester grabbed another book.

"Not again," I mumbled.

"Fine, I won't read it," Chester said. "The writing is garbage, anyway."

Howie gasped at this literary assessment.

"Don't Go in the Yard," Chester went on. "Know it, Howie?"

"Know it? It's a classic!"

"And do you remember what's in the yard?"

"Grass?" Howie guessed. "Buried bones?"

"Think, Howie."

"Oh, right. Birds. Wait, not just any birds. Crows!"

"That's right, Howie. Crows. Bad crows. Not nice crows. Really mean crows. And who, I wonder, do those bad, not nice, really mean crows go after? Surely not Skippy Sapworthy."

Howie thought for a moment. And then a shiver went through him. "No," he said, "you're right, Pop. It isn't Skippy Sapworthy. It's his dog, Binky-Boy. He's transformed into a scarecrow!"

"The pets," Chester intoned. "It's always the pets."

Suddenly There Came a Tapping

The next three weeks passed uneventfully, unless you want to count Chester's chronic state of hysteria as an event. I will spare you the details, because to be honest, I couldn't bear having to relive them myself. Suffice it to say that he spent the wee hours of many a night at Mr. Monroe's computer doing what he insisted on calling "research," creating pie charts and spreadsheets on such topics as "The Different Methods Used in the Flesh-Crawlers Series to Transform Household Pets into Unspeakable Monstrosities" and "Common Denominators Among Crows, Authors of Juvenile Horror Fiction, and Kitchen Appliances." I never really understood that one. I think it had something to do with the "fact" (Chester's word) that most of the household pets in the FleshCrawlers books were transformed into unspeakable monstrosities with the aid of kitchen appliances.

By the time our guests were to arrive, Chester was so tightly strung you could have used him to hang out laundry. I'm not sure how he thought his "research" was going to be of any help, but he insisted it was crucial preparation.

The other members of the household were busy preparing as well. Every day Pete came home from school with reports of all that was being done to get ready for the famous author's visit. He also reported that no one was making fun of him any longer for liking M. T. Graves. From the way he told it, winning this contest had turned him into some kind of hero. Of course, Pete often talks about himself in heroic terms, so it was hard to know if what he was saying was true or not. Kyle was back to being Pete's best friend and had even made the welcome banner for our front yard. Pete and Toby were rereading the entire FleshCrawlers series, which had Howie running back and forth between their rooms, trying to keep up.

Mr. and Mrs. Monroe were busy getting the house ready and worrying about having everything just right for their important visitor. Apparently they'd been given some specific—and rather puzzling—instructions.

"I've never known a houseguest to e-mail a list of requests before," I heard Mr. Monroe say to his wife one day as he was making a dessert. I just happened to be in the kitchen at the time in case any assistance was needed in protecting the floor from falling ingredients.

"And such odd requests, too," said Mrs. Monroe. "He asks for Bunnicula to stay in his room with him."

"That's not so odd," Mr. Monroe said as he stirred something that was making my salivary glands salivate. "After all, he said he was interested in spending some quality time with the pets."

"Yes, but what about this?" Mrs. Monroe went on, consulting a piece of paper. "'Salad—without dressing—to be available at all hours. And a plate of lettuce to be placed by my bed for a midnight snack.'"

Mr. Monroe laughed. "Well, I can't say it's my idea of a midnight snack, but to each his own. I guess he's just a bit eccentric."

Or out of his mind, I could imagine Chester saying. But then who was Chester to talk? He's been out of his mind so long he'd need a map to find his way back.

On the afternoon M. T. Graves was to arrive, I was deeply engrossed in preparations of my own when I felt a tapping on my eyelids.

"Chester?" I said. "If that's you, stop it at once. I need my sleep."

"You always need your sleep," Chester replied, even while continuing his annoying habit of knocking at my eyelids to wake me up. I hate when he does this, especially when it's been a while since his nails have been clipped.

"Yes, but I need it even more now," I told him,

being careful not to sound too alert. "It's important to be well rested when you have guests coming."

"This is how you're preparing? By napping?"

I nodded, which quickly led to nodding *off*. Chester picked up the pace of his eyelid batting. "Well, I've been preparing, too," he told me.

"Please," I begged, "no more Venn diagrams."

Chester snorted. "I've been engaged in serious research," he said.

"You've been engaged in serious research for three weeks, Chester, and all we've learned so far is to stay away from the toaster oven. Well, it just so happens that I've been engaged in research, too. I was dreaming about bacon, and I was about to determine how many slices I could eat before getting a tummyache. I was up to one hundred and fourteen."

Suddenly Chester was on top of me, playing my eyeballs like a set of drums.

"Stop!" I woofed, shaking him off and opening my poor, battered eyes. I couldn't believe how bright the room was, considering that the sky outside was decidedly gloomy. "You didn't happen to bring any coffee with you, did you?"

Chester glared at me. "I'm trying to be serious here, Harold," he said.

"I just thought—"

"Yes, well, think about this," he said. I sensed he was not about to ask if I wanted cinnamon with my cappuccino. "I did some more research on M. T. Graves last night, and I'm telling you, the guy is deranged."

"That's nice. It will give you something in common."

"Go ahead, Harold. Mock, ridicule, sneer, deride, disdain . . ."

"Okay, okay," I said. Chester has a fondness for the thesaurus that can be exhausting. "Why is he deranged? And please tell me your answer doesn't involve a spreadsheet."

"One," Chester began, consulting the spreadsheet in his head, "his favorite fish is the piranha. When asked why, he said—and I quote—'They are good eaters, leaving neither crumbs nor evidence behind.' 'Evidence,' Harold? A curious word, don't you think? Unless, of course, one is thinking about . . . *crime*!

"Two, he was raised by his grandparents because his parents were never home. Why, you may ask?"

Or not, I thought.

"Because they were spies! The only contact

Graves had with them during his entire childhood was a single postcard sent from a dungeon in Bora-Bora!"

I shook my head, hoping to give the appearance of amazement while in fact merely attempting to stay awake.

"And get this," Chester went on. "When asked how he likes to spend his free time, he replied, 'I enjoy baking, playing with my chemistry set, and training my bats. Oh, and I do like to have a go at sorcery from time to time.' Sorcery, Harold! Chemistry experiments! Bat training! What more do you need to know?"

"What sorts of things does he like to bake?" I inquired.

Chester didn't answer me. He was on a roll and there was no getting him off it. "And what about this crow of his?" he ranted. "Do we think it's a coincidence that he's named for Edgar Allan Poe?"

"Who?" I asked.

"Edgar Allan Poe, the greatest writer of horror fiction of all time. Poe also wrote poems. Surely you have heard of his poem 'The Raven.'"

Before I could ask him why he was calling me

Shirley, Chester narrowed his eyes and launched into a throaty recitation:

> *Once upon a midnight dreary, while I*
>   *pondered, weak and weary,*
> *Over many a quaint and curious volume*
>   *of forgotten lore—*
> *While I nodded, nearly napping, suddenly*
>   *there came a tapping,*
> *As of some one gently rapping, rapping at*
>   *my chamber door.*
> *"'Tis some visitor," I muttered, "tapping at*
>   *my chamber door—*
> *Only this and nothing more."*

"I like the part about napping," I told him. "And the tapping part reminds me of a certain someone who has a problem with a certain other someone getting his minimum daily requirement of sleep. But I can't say I really see your point."

"My *point*," Chester snapped, "is that in the poem the visitor on the other side of the door is a *raven*, Harold! Which is more or less a crow. And this raven has only one thing to say."

"Corn?" I conjectured.

"'Nevermore,'" said Chester. "To every question, every plea, every desperate cry, the answer is always the same: 'Nevermore.' A word that like the raven itself serves as an omen foretelling a desolate descent into darkness."

"That's some word," I commented as Howie raced into the room and put an end to our conversation.

"M. T. Graves will be here any minute!" he exclaimed. "How do I look?"

Chester peered at Howie through half-closed lids. "You look like a wirehaired dachshund puppy," he said. "How do you *think* you look?"

"Is my hair okay?"

"No, Howie, you'd better call your stylist for an emergency trim."

Howie began to panic. "Really, Pop? I don't know if she can fit me in. I think it's her afternoon to go to her shiatsu massage therapist. Or maybe she takes her Shih Tzu for a sausage hairpiece. It's a little hard to understand what she says sometimes. I think it's because she chews gum and she's got that blower thing going right next to my ear and—"

"YOUR HAIR LOOKS FINE!" Chester shouted.

For the record, Howie does not have a stylist. What he has is a very active imagination.

All at once there was the most alarming racket coming from our backyard. It sounded like the caws of a thousand crows. When we ran to look out the dining room window, my speculation was confirmed. There, filling the yard like a black cloud, were more crows than I'd ever seen in one place, screeching raucously as they swooped from tree to tree. Their presence made the dark sky even darker.

Howie's eyes grew as wide as water bowls. "Don't go in the yard," I heard him mutter as the Monroes came running in.

"What's going on?" Toby asked. I felt his hand reach for the top of my head.

"I don't know. I've never seen anything like this," said Mr. Monroe.

The din outside was so deafening we didn't even hear the other alarming noise at first. Who knows how long it had been going on?

Then it seemed we all heard it at the same time, turning as one and staring wide-eyed at the front door. From the other side of the door, there came a tapping.

"We should answer it," said Mrs. Monroe.

But no one moved.

FOUR

A Fine Murder
of Crows

It's M. T. Graves," Pete said at last. "I'll get it."
He was trying to sound brave, but the tremor in his voice gave him away.

"Yes," Mrs. Monroe said, looking a little dazed. "M. T. Graves. We mustn't keep him waiting."

The tapping grew more urgent as Pete made his way to the door. He reached for the handle and slowly began to turn it. The shrieking of the crows and the beating of their frantic wings—not to mention Howie's rapid-fire panting next to me—provided an eerie soundtrack.

The handle turned. The latch clicked. The door creaked open.

And there on the other side stood . . . Kyle.

"What took you so long? Is he here yet? When are you going to get your doorbell fixed? What's up with all the crows in your backyard? Oh, hi, Mr. and Mrs. Monroe. What's everybody staring at? Why does Howie look like he's going to pass out? Did you know your cat's eyes are bugging out of his head? So, is M. T. Graves here or what?"

Kyle likes to talk.

Pete opened his mouth to answer his friend when he suddenly fell speechless. We all did. Even Howie stopped his panting. For there, behind Kyle, loomed a tall—a *very* tall—figure in black. Black pupils stared down at us from eyes that bulged beneath bushy black eyebrows. Long black hair fell on either side of an ashen white face to meet a black cape that was draped around stooped shoulders. On one of those shoulders sat a large black bird, who regarded us with bright, unblinking eyes.

"That's a . . . fine . . . murder . . . of crows," the gigantic figure said in a low voice that stopped and started and rumbled like distant thunder.

"A m-m-murder of crows, did you say?" Mrs. Monroe sputtered. In all the years I've known her,

I've never heard Mrs. Monroe sputter. She's a lawyer. Lawyers don't sputter.

"A flock of crows is also called a 'murder,'" Mr. Monroe explained. "Isn't that right?"

The tall, spooky-looking man nodded as Chester muttered, "Interesting choice of words."

"Please come in," said Mrs. Monroe, now sputter-free. "Forgive our lack of manners. This racket is unnerving."

Kyle tilted his head back in order to gaze up at the stranger who was entering the house. "Are you M. T. Graves?" he asked. "Is that the real Edgar Allan Crow up there? He won't peck out my eyes, will he? Did you notice the welcome sign out front? I made it. I'm sorry it's not better. I'm not very good at art stuff. I'm Kyle. I don't live here."

"Hello, Kyle," the tall man rumbled. Turning to Mr. and Mrs. Monroe, he asked, "May I . . . sit?"

"Of course," said Mr. Monroe. "You've had a long trip. Do you have any bags?"

Lowering himself with a heavy sigh into Chester's chair (well, the chair that Chester *calls* his), the man in black waved vaguely toward the front door. "They're . . . in the car," he said. "Might I have a glass of . . . water?"

"I'll get it!" Pete volunteered.

He was out of the room and back with a glass of water before you could say, "Behold the powers of darkness." Unless of course you were Chester, in which case you could say it twice.

"Here you go, Mr. Graves," said Pete.

"It's Tanner," said the stranger, offering his companion a few sips before downing the remainder of the glass in a single swallow.

"But I thought—"

"M. T. Graves is my nom de plume."

"Your *what*?" Kyle asked.

"My pen name, the name I use for writing. My real name is Miles Tanner."

"Oh, okay. Well, I'm Pete. And this is my mom and dad. And you met Kyle, and that runt over there is Toby."

"Hey!"

"Well, you are!"

"Boys!"

Pete rolled his eyes. "Whatever. Oh, and these are our pets. You want to meet *them*, right? Because you said in your letter . . ."

Scowling, Miles Tanner clenched his hands into fists and pulled himself back into the chair. It wasn't quite the enthusiastic greeting I was expecting. "Yes . . . certainly . . . but perhaps another—"

Pete grabbed my collar and dragged me over to the brown velvet armchair. "This is Harold," he told the author. "Be careful he doesn't drool on you."

Before I could register a complaint, Pete went on, "And that's Chester. Watch out for him. He's totally . . ." He put his finger near his ear and made a circular motion.

Chester hissed.

"See?" Pete said.

Howie couldn't stand it any longer. He began yipping a mile a minute. Loosely translated, his yips went something like this: *Hey! What about me? I'm your biggest fan in the entire universe! I've read every one of your books!* Screaming Mummies of the Pharaoh's Tomb *is the best book in the entire universe! I want to be just like you when I grow up! Don't you think I'd make an excellent character for one of your books? Aren't I cute? Hey! What about me?*

Miles Tanner's only response to Howie's tirade was to cover his ears and say, "Make him stop . . . please."

Crushed, Howie stopped yipping immediately.

"I'm sorry," said Mrs. Monroe. "He's a puppy. He's easily excited."

"That's Howie for you," said Pete. "I'll bet he was barking at Edgar. He's got this thing about crows."

"Pete," said Mr. Monroe, "why don't you take the animals out of the room for a few minutes? Let's give our guest a chance to catch his breath."

"Well, I never!" Chester exclaimed after Pete had unceremoniously dumped us in the kitchen. "'Take the *animals* out of the room'? Ex-cu-u-u-use me!"

"M. T. Graves *hates* me," Howie moaned. "Why did I have to yip so much? And why did Pete have to say I was barking at Edgar?"

"I'm telling you," Chester said, "there is something *wrong* with this picture. We've got to find out what it is."

"What are you talking about now?" I asked.

"What am I talking about now? What am I talking about *now*? What am *I* talking about now? What *am* I talking—"

"I believe that was the question."

"What I'm talking about is, this is the man who is supposed to love animals so much. But look at him! He couldn't care less—except for that weird bird on his shoulder. What a creepy twosome *they* make! I'm telling you, he just wants to use us, Harold. We've got to be on our toes the whole time he's in this house, do you understand?"

"I *can't* be on my toes the whole time, Pop," Howie whined. "I'll tip over."

Chester grimaced. "Why do I waste my . . . wait a minute, we're wasting time right now! Follow me."

Against my better judgment, I followed Chester out of the kitchen and down the hall to where we were within earshot of the conversation going on in the living room.

"And tomorrow we're planning a lunch in your honor," Mrs. Monroe was saying. "There will be a few guests. The principal. Pete's English teacher, of course. The librarian."

"Ms. Pickles," Kyle put in. "That's her name. She has to spend the first two weeks of school every year getting the new kids not to laugh when they say it. It's pretty funny, though, right? I mean, not that it's right to laugh at somebody's name, but you kind of can't help laughing when you say 'pickles,' especially when it's a person's name. Try it. You'll see what I'm talking about. Anyway, she's really nice. You'll like her. Not that I know who you'll like or anything, but . . . oh, and just wait until you see how many of your books are in the library. Hey, what are you going to talk about when you come to our school? Did you bring pictures of your wolves and bats and—"

Mrs. Monroe cleared her throat. "Thank you, Kyle. Now, let's see, did I leave anyone out?"

"I'm not doing anything tomorrow," Kyle said.

"Well, Kyle, would you like to join us?" Mrs. Monroe asked politely. "We'll be eating at twelve thirty."

"Wow, could I, Mrs. Monroe? That would be awesome. You don't really drink blood, do you, Mr. Graves . . . I mean, Mr. Tanner? Because I read somewhere that you do, and I gotta tell you, the sight of blood kind of grosses me out. Nothing personal."

Mrs. Monroe laughed nervously. This was something else I'd never heard her do before. "I'm sure Mr. Tanner doesn't drink blood, Kyle," she said.

"Good," said Kyle. "I mean, it's a free country and all, but—"

"Oh, could Amber come, too?" Pete asked.

"Ooh, Amber, your *girlfriend*," Toby said.

"She is *not*."

47

"She is *so*. Everybody says."

"Boys! Mr. Tanner, I'm sorry, I can see this is getting to be too much. Kyle is welcome to join us, Pete, but no more guests, okay? Mr. Tanner, are you all right? You look a little . . ."

"Tired," the low voice rumbled. "May I . . . lie down?"

"Of course," said Mrs. Monroe. "We'll show you to your room. Dinner will be in an hour. And it will just be the family tonight, no guests. We'll be having my husband's vegetarian lasagna and salad with no dressing, just the way you asked."

"But—" Tanner began.

"Oh, and Bunnicula is up in your room," said Mr. Monroe.

"Just the way you asked," Pete said.

"In my room? But won't he be—"

Tanner's words were cut off by the sound of wings flapping as Edgar suddenly flew from his shoulders and began circling the room.

"Edgar!" Tanner cried out. "Come back here!"

Edgar continued to fly about the room. His beak opened and closed, but no sound came out. His eerie silence was offset by the loud and somehow threatening caws of the crows outside.

"What on *earth* is going on?" Mr. Monroe asked.

"Hey, Dad," said Pete, "this is like that movie, *The Birds*. Remember?"

"I saw that movie," Kyle chimed in. "We'd better board up the windows before the crows get inside and peck out our eyes. Maybe we should wear goggles. Or helmets. Mr. Monroe, do you have any plywood?"

Strangely, Chester wasn't paying any attention to the commotion. "Howie," he said, "you've got to run up to the guest room and hide under the bed."

"Say what?"

"You heard me. You've got to hide under the bed. You're the only one who will fit."

"You'll fit, Pop."

"Yes, but I'm needed at Command Central."

"Ah," said Howie. "In that case, okay."

Chester often says things like "I'm needed at Command Central" to get Howie to do what he wants.

"We've got to spy on those two," Chester went on. "We can't let them out of our sight. I don't know what they're up to, but I'm going to find out. And you're the one who's going to do the finding out for me!"

"Awesome!" said Howie, as if Chester had just pinned a junior detective badge on him.

"Hurry, while everyone is distracted!"

"Okay, Pop, I'm going. Gee, maybe I'll overhear some writing tips. Would that be okay?"

"Fine, fine. Whatever. But don't get so hung up on adjectives that you miss the important stuff."

"What's an adjective?" Howie asked.

"A describing word," Chester explained. "Now get moving."

Howie pondered this. "Oh, like in the sentence, 'Howie is a funny, smart, and cute-as-a-button puppy,' the words 'funny', 'smart', and 'cute-as-a-button' are adjectives?"

Chester rolled his eyes. "Something like that," he said. "Now would you please—"

"I've never understood what's so cute about buttons," I interjected.

"Would you *please* get going?" Chester implored Howie as he glowered at me.

"I'm gone," Howie said. And he scampered up the stairs and out of sight.

"Once again, Chester," I said, "you are making a case out of nothing. Other than Miles Tanner being a little peculiar . . ."

"Not just him. What about the bird? What's up with the silent treatment?"

"Maybe he has laryngitis," I suggested, thinking how nice it would be if Chester had laryngitis on occasion.

"Maybe he does," Chester replied. "And maybe when he gets his voice back, the first thing he will say is—"

"'Nevermore.' I know. But a bunch of maybes is all you've got, Chester. What *evidence* do you have that Tanner is up to anything?"

Chester began to bathe his tail.

"Aha!" I said. "You don't have *any* evidence, do you?"

"May we help you get your bags from the car?" I heard Mr. Monroe ask as everyone entered the hallway where Chester and I were lurking about. Edgar had returned to his master's shoulder, and the crows outside had quieted down.

"Thank you," the author replied. "But leave the black bag with the silver clasp. I'll . . . bring that one . . . in."

"It's okay, we can get everything, Mr. Tanner," said Kyle. "I'm strong. I've been working out. Between Pete and me, we can—"

"NO!" Miles Tanner boomed. Immediately dropping his voice, he said, "I'm sorry, but . . . I'll fetch . . . the black bag . . . myself."

So shocked that he forgot to take his tail out of his mouth, Chester turned to me and asked, "Wath it evidenth you were after, Harold?"

FIVE

The Odd Guest

No one said another word as Mr. Monroe opened the door and led the way to the car. Mr. Tanner's cape flapped noisily in the wind before us. I didn't want to tell Chester, but I have to confess that in that moment I began to find something a little scary about this tall, stooped-shouldered figure with his dark eyes and pale skin. Based on his appearance alone, it was easy to think him guilty until proven innocent. Guilty of *what* seemed almost beside the point.

When we reached the car (a surprisingly modest, nondescript box on wheels parked haphazardly at the curb), Mr. Tanner immediately grabbed the black bag in the backseat and clutched it to him. Kyle, Pete, and Toby fought over the two suitcases in the trunk and somehow managed to get them out without destroying them.

Tanner's attachment to his black bag was strange enough, but then something even stranger occurred. It was as we turned to go back inside that a single crow appeared over the roof of the house and came to rest on a tree branch above the living room window. It opened its beak and let out a cry that was at once plaintive and rallying. Edgar took off immediately, even as Tanner dropped the black bag and grabbed for him.

We all watched as Edgar flew up to land next to the bird on the branch. He appeared to bow before the other crow, and this gesture was repeated several times. Then the sky above the house grew dark with black wings as what looked like hundreds of crows flew up from behind the house and landed on the roof.

We stared for a moment in silence.

"I've never seen so many crows in one place," said Mrs. Monroe at last.

"We have a flock that roosts in our backyard," Mr. Monroe commented, "but this is twice that number at least."

"It's the same at . . . my place," said Mr. Tanner. "I don't live very far . . . from here, you know. These crows . . . I think they've . . . followed us here."

"Is that possible?" Mr. Monroe asked. "Could they have flown all this way?"

No one had an answer for that. Except Chester, of course. He muttered under his breath, "Anything is possible when dark forces reign."

I was all set to say, "Chester, knock it off," until I thought of Tanner's cape flapping in the wind, the blackness of his eyes that seemed to go on forever, the unsettling rumble of his voice, and I kept silent.

When Tanner called out to Edgar this time, it was less a command than a plea. "Edgar, come back. Won't you . . . please?"

Edgar bowed one last time to the other crow, then flew back to Tanner and nipped him lightly on the ear.

"Ah, my dear friend," Tanner said with a deep sigh as he stroked Edgar's feathers.

Returning to the house, Chester mumbled, "It's all theater, Harold."

"Beg pardon?"

"It's all a big performance. Edgar and this Tanner or Graves or whoever he really is. They're putting on a show to dazzle us so that we'll be blind to their terrible deeds when they finally strike."

"But what was Edgar doing up there with that other crow?" I asked.

"I'm not sure, but I'll figure it out. There's no pulling the wool over this cat's eyes. Oh, no, my friend. I am too smart for the likes of — ow!"

Chester had been so busy talking he hadn't noticed the door swing shut in front of us.

"Is your nose okay?" I asked. "I guess we'll have to go around and use the pet door."

"By dose is fide," he told me, which I took to mean he was all right.

After our guest had finished napping and Howie had confessed that he, too, had napped when he should have been spying from under the bed (I believe his exact words were, "Who knew the carpeting in the guest room was so comfy?"), the family gathered for dinner.

Miles, as he asked the Monroes to call him, got the conversational ball rolling by announcing in that rumbly, spooky voice of his that Edgar was still resting in his cage and that Bunnicula was "an interesting, if sleepy, specimen of a rabbit."

Chester mouthed the word "specimen" at me from his place under the table. I wasn't sure what his point was, but he explained it later when he presented the evidence he was accumulating in the case of *The People* (aka Chester) *versus Miles Tanner* (aka M. T. Graves, the Madman Who Could Turn Us into Mutants with the Aid of Waffle Irons). Lucky for me Chester didn't get his paws on a computer, or we would have been swimming in spreadsheets.

"Ordinarily, I do not keep Edgar in a . . . cage," Miles went on. "But I thought he might be more comfortable for now, since he is in a new and . . . unfamiliar . . . place. Might I set him . . . free . . . later?"

"Of course," said Mr. Monroe.

"Is Bunnicula . . . allowed out of his . . . cage?" Miles asked then. I noticed Chester's ears perk up. "I would love to . . . get to . . . know him."

"We don't let him run loose," Mrs. Monroe said, "but of course you may take him out of his cage."

"Excellent," said Miles. "I want to see those eyes that glow in the dark . . . up close. How thoughtful of you to . . . put his cage . . . in my room."

Mr. and Mrs. Monroe exchanged a glance. I knew

what they were thinking: Miles had *asked* to have Bunnicula's cage kept in his room.

"Would you please pass the . . . salad dressing?" Miles asked then, and the Monroes exchanged another look.

How strange, I thought. Hadn't Miles specifically requested salad *without* dressing?

After dinner, I overheard Mr. and Mrs. Monroe quietly discussing their odd guest in the kitchen, while Miles sat in the living room talking Flesh-Crawlers with Pete and Toby. Needless to say, Howie was in there too, hanging on each word and using everything in his power to keep from yipping.

When Chester and I sauntered in, Miles's face contracted like a washcloth being wrung out. His hands tightened their grip on his knees. I began to think that Miles could give Chester a real run for his money in the "tightly wound" department. Toby and Pete didn't seem to notice as they grilled him with their questions.

"Where do you get all the ideas for your books?" Toby was asking.

Miles darted a few looks our way, then said, "Life."

"You mean all those things have *happened* to you?" Toby asked.

"In a . . . way," said Miles.

Pete snorted. "No offense, Mr. Tanner, but most of the stuff you write about couldn't happen to anybody. That's why it's called fantasy."

Toby reached across Miles and jabbed his brother's knee. "Says who?" he asked. "Mr. Tanner practices *sorcery*. Did you forget that? And what about his bats? What about your bats, Mr. Tanner? Are they *vampire* bats? And what's it like living with wolves? You must really love animals, huh? I wish you could have brought all your pets with you. Hey, maybe we could visit *you* sometime!"

Howie panted enthusiastically to show his support of that idea.

"Oh, well, I don't know about . . . that." Miles squirmed uncomfortably as he looked over at Chester and me.

"Do you think they . . . need to go out?" he asked, indicating with a nod of his head that Howie, Chester, and I were the "they" to whom he was referring.

Pete shrugged. "They use the pet door when they go out. Why? Do you want to take them for a walk?"

Toby chimed in, "Cool idea. Let's go for a walk,

Mr. Tanner. Maybe Edgar could go with us."

"No!" Miles said emphatically. "We don't need to go for a walk. I just . . . perhaps I should go upstairs to let Edgar out of his cage. If he's in it too long, it becomes a . . . prison . . . to him."

I was struck anew by the way Miles spoke. It wasn't just that his voice was low and rumbly. It was that he spoke slowly and haltingly, as though every word were an effort. And no matter what he was talking about, he sounded sad. It came to me later that the word I was looking for, the word that fit Miles Tanner perfectly, was "melancholy."

"Can we go with you?" Toby asked. "To let Edgar out of his cage, I mean? Bunnicula should be up by now. He wakes up when it gets dark."

"So he is a . . . creature of the . . . night," said Miles.

"I guess," Toby said.

"You can see how his eyes glow in the dark," said Pete. "It's way cool."

"Yes," said Miles, raising his hands slowly upward and rubbing them together. "Yes, that would . . . interest me. Very . . . much."

As the threesome made its way up the stairs, Chester turned to me with one eyebrow arched. I knew that meant he was about to speak at some length. I looked for the nearest exit, but he got started before I could escape.

"I have it all figured out," he began.

"Does that mean we have the rest of the night off?" I asked.

"Hardly. We must be ever vigilant, Harold, you know that. This is a man who used the word 'specimen' to describe Bunnicula. Unusual word, don't you think? Unless you're a scientist—a *mad* scientist, perhaps—who sees a living being not as a living being but as fodder for some gene-altering experiment!"

"I heard Mrs. Monroe say she had to get her jeans altered because she was getting fodder," said Howie.

Chester glared at Howie.

"Okay, not really," Howie said. "But that was a good one, right? Am I right?"

Chester replied, "Howie, if you call the radio station and you're the one hundredth caller they'll give you a one-way paid vacation to the Bahamas."

"Really?"

"Absolutely."

Howie left the room.

"That was cruel," I said.

"Think of it as pest control. Now, where was I? Ah, yes: Tanner's interest in Bunnicula. Do you notice that he practically recoils at the sight of the rest of us? That's because he's afraid we'll get in his way. It's Bunnicula he's after, Harold, there's no doubt of it. And did you notice how Edgar and Tanner were all lovey-dovey after Edgar flew up to the top of that tree branch and met with the head crow?"

"The head what?"

"The head crow. You saw how Edgar went up there and was bowing all over the place. Edgar and Miles are in cahoots with some kind of crow crime family."

"Oh, yeah," I said. "That makes a whole lot of sense."

"The evidence speaks for itself. Tanner is full of lies, and the two of them are full of charades. And Edgar has to be out of his cage so that he can fly out and consult with the head crow. I rest my case."

Oh, if only Chester did rest his case. If only he would *ever* rest his case.

"I don't know," I said, "you may have a case . . . or half a case . . . about Miles, but Edgar seems like a regular crow to me."

"So-called 'regular crows' are anything but regular,

Harold. They are very clever and resourceful crea-
tures. They know how to fashion tools to get to
their food, they play games of their own invention,
and they're excellent mimics. Other than their unfortunate taste for roadkill, there's a lot to admire in
them. However, as much as one might be tempted to
respect their intelligence, one must remember that
above all else, crows are crafty."

Chester's research was finally beginning to interest
me. "Crafty?" I asked. "Do you think Edgar might
be able to knit me some socks for the winter?"

Chester stared blankly at me.

"My feet get cold," I explained. "They didn't used
to, but as I get older, I find—"

"Harold! 'Crafty' as in 'sly,' not 'crafty' as in
'pinecone bird feeders'!"

"Ah," I said, although I didn't see what pinecone
bird feeders had to do with anything. And I still
needed socks.

"Besides, Harold, you're forgetting that there is
something that makes Edgar anything but a regular
crow."

I thought about it. "He doesn't like corn?" I ven-
tured.

"He never makes a sound," said Chester. "Unless

of course that too is all an act. There's so much for us to find out. It's a good thing Howie is going to spend the night under the bed. And this time he had better stay awake!"

"Aren't you worried about him?" I asked. "What if we wake up in the morning and he's been transformed into a steel-plated gummy bear?"

"I can assure you, Harold, that we do not have to worry about Howie. It's Bunnicula they're interested in. It's Bunnicula they're after."

Just then, Howie came racing into the room. "Guess what!" he exclaimed. "I was the ninety-ninth caller! I didn't win the trip to the Bahamas, but I did win a nice set of Samsonite luggage! I'm going to share it with you, Pop. Do you want the carry-on tote or the garment bag?"

Chester was spared being drawn into Howie's Wonderful World of the Imagination by a very real knock on the door. Mr. Monroe appeared from the kitchen to answer it.

"Good evening," said a woman's voice.

"Ms. Pickles," said Mr. Monroe. "What a nice surprise."

"I hope you don't mind my stopping by like this," the school librarian said.

"Not at all," Mr. Monroe said. "Please come in."

"Well, only for a moment," said the tall, frizzy-haired woman in a long, chocolate brown cape who entered. She was holding a covered dish in both hands. "I didn't have room in my refrigerator," she explained, holding the dish out to Mr. Monroe. "It's a pretzel crust Jell-O mold . . . for lunch tomorrow. The recipe called for strawberries, but I used pineapple chunks instead. It's so hard to find good strawberries this time of year, and besides . . ."

"Besides, I adore pineapple chunks," came a rumbly voice from the top of the stairs.

The librarian nearly dropped her mold when she looked up and beheld the author of the Flesh-Crawlers series gazing down at her. Edgar was perched on his shoulder, and Pete and Toby stood on either side of him.

"Mr. Graves, I presume," she said.

"It's Tanner, actually. And you must be . . ."

"Ms. Pickles!" Pete cried. "Remember, I was telling you about her?" He poked Miles in the leg, presumably to remind him not to giggle at Ms. Pickles's name.

"You were talking about me?" The librarian's cheeks flushed. "I am honored. And please call me

Marjorie." She extended her arm as if to shake his hand.

"The honor is mine, and you must call me Miles," said Miles as he descended the stairs. Edgar flew down ahead of him and alighted on Ms. Pickles's extended arm.

"Oh!" she said. "How lovely. Is this . . . ?"

"Edgar Allan Crow," Miles Tanner said, as he approached and took Ms. Pickles's hand in his own. "We were just upstairs saying hello to Pete's unusual pet, Bunnicula."

"I would say this is a house full of unusual pets," said Ms. Pickles. "A fact that delights me, lover of animals that I am. Though it does make me sad to see a wild bird in captivity. Oh, I'm sorry, I hope I didn't offend you."

"It would be impossible for you to offend anyone," Miles said. I noticed he was speaking without hesitation and that he didn't sound as melancholy. I wondered if the change was due to his adoration of pineapples.

As if reading my mind, he said, "I not only adore pineapples, I'm wild for pretzel crusts. How did you know?"

"Your website," Ms. Pickles confessed.

"How remarkable that you found a truth among so many lies," Miles said mysteriously.

Edgar fluttered his wings, startling the librarian into a fit of nervous laughter and erasing Miles's curious comment from everyone's mind.

Everyone's mind but Chester's, that is. It was he who proposed that Miles and Edgar existed in a tangle of mysteries, where lies and truths made up a web of deception in which to catch the innocent and unwary.

I would have accused him of overreacting, were it not for a cry in the night—and the disappearance of not one unusual pet . . . but *two*.

SIX

It's in the Bag

It was shortly before dawn when the cry of "Edgar!" woke the entire household from its slumber. It was Miles's voice, but seconds later Toby's voice joined in with, "Bunnicula's missing, too!"

I quickly made my way upstairs from the kitchen, where I'd spent the night (I wanted to be first in line for Mr. Monroe's famous pancakes, which had been promised for Sunday morning breakfast).

"But how could they get out?" Mr. Monroe asked as he rubbed sleep from his eyes.

Miles was shaking his head. His complexion, pallid to begin with, had become white as bone. "I

69

don't . . . know. I . . . don't . . . know," he repeated. "I got up to use the . . . you know . . . and . . . when I got back I saw they were both missing."

"They must still be in the house somewhere," said Mr. Monroe. "Let's look for them."

I started following the family, when Chester caught my tail in his teeth. I hate when he does that.

"Come on, Chester," I said. "We've got to help them look."

"Of course we do," Chester agreed, after he'd dropped my tail. "But first let's check in with our spy, shall we?"

Howie! *He* would know what had happened!

We entered the guest room and found Howie sound asleep under the bed.

"Howie! Wake up!" Chester ordered.

Howie's eyes popped open. "Is it morning?" he asked groggily. He then sneezed. A dust bunny landed several inches from his nose.

"Howie, get out from under there and tell us everything you know!" Chester demanded.

"Okay, Pop." Howie wriggled his way out from under the bed and cleared his throat. "My name is Howie," he began. "I live with Mr. and Mrs. Monroe and their two sons, Toby and Pete, in the town of Centerville. My best friends are Chester and Harold, whom I call Pop and Uncle Harold. The capital of the United States is Washington, D.C. Two plus two equals four. Never wear plaids and stripes together. The average dog should have its ears checked once a week to see if they need cleaning. However, dogs with long, pendulous ears, such as those of a basset hound, should be checked more—"

"HOWIE!" Chester shouted. "I am asking what you know about Bunnicula's disappearance!"

"Oh," said Howie. "Did Bunnicula disappear?"

Chester gnashed his teeth.

"You really shouldn't do that, Pop," Howie pointed out. "It wears down the enamel."

"Howie!"

"What? It's something else I know."

"Howie," I said. "Did you notice Bunnicula getting out during the night?"

Howie looked down at the floor. "Well, I didn't exactly stay . . . you know . . . exactly . . ."

"Awake?" Chester speculated. "Is that the word you're searching for?"

"Kind of," said Howie. "But I did hear some stuff before I fell asleep."

"Fine," said Chester. "Give us a full report, and then we've got to start looking for Bunnicula."

Howie's face took on a look of deep concentration. "Okay," he began, "first of all, before Miles went to bed he went over to Bunnicula's cage and started talking to him."

Chester's eyes lit up. "What did he say?"

"He said, 'Nice bunny.'"

"That's it? 'Nice bunny'?"

"No, then he said, 'Twitchy-nose bunny.'"

"Ooh," I said. "I'll bet that's mad scientist code for—"

"You're skating on thin ice, Harold," Chester warned. "Go on, Howie."

"Well, he just talked to him like that for a while. You know, sort of baby bunny talk. Oh, at one point, he said, 'You're a rabbit, you're okay.' Then he took this deep breath—I mean, it was so loud I could hear it all the way under the bed—and then he was quiet."

Chester snorted. "'You're a rabbit, you're okay.' What does that mean? Did he take Bunnicula out of his cage?"

"I don't know. I don't think so, but I couldn't see. It didn't *sound* like he took him out of his cage. All I heard after that was the sound of typing."

"Typing?"

Howie got really excited telling this part of the story. "Uh-huh. He was writing, Pop! Can you believe it? My hero, M. T. Graves, was *writing* right here in this very room!"

I looked over at the laptop computer sitting on the dresser. I knew what Chester was going to say before he said it.

"No, Chester," I said. "We are not going to break into his computer."

Chester rolled his eyes as if the thought would never have crossed his mind.

"I was so inspired," Howie went on. "I mean it. I couldn't fall asleep for *seconds* I was so full of story ideas. I have this one idea that is so cool. It's about this dog who has fleas, except it turns out they're not ordinary fleas, see, they're steel-plated *Crypto-Fleas* and they've been sent from another—"

"Howie!" said Chester. "I'll listen to your ideas another time, okay?"

"Really, Pop?"

"Well, no. But Harold will, won't you, Harold? Right now what I need to hear is what else happened with Miles and Edgar and Bunnicula."

"Oh, well, while he was typing he was muttering

things that I couldn't really hear. And then he was quiet for a long time. And then he was muttering again, and then I heard him say, 'I can't do it alone, Edgar. You've got to help me.'"

"Help him what?" Chester asked suspiciously.

"I don't know. He stopped talking. A few minutes later the bed sagged, and soon after that the snoring began. And that's when I had all my story ideas, and then I fell asleep."

"That's it?" said Chester. "That's the whole report?"

Howie thought for a moment, and then his eyes lit up. "Wait, there *is* something else! Before he went to bed, Miles opened the window. He said something about it being stuffy in here. Then he went over and picked up the black bag—"

Chester gasped. "The black bag!"

"Uh-huh. He got the black bag and took it to bed with him."

"He took it to bed with him? Okay, that's just weird."

"I know. I woke up at one point and took a peek around the room. Edgar and Bunnicula were asleep. So was Miles—and he was *hugging* the black bag."

"And *that* is even weirder," said Chester as he

raised himself up to peer over the top of the bed.

"There it is," he said. "There's our answer."

"Where?" I asked.

"In the bag, Harold. It probably holds the tools of his villainous trade."

Chester jumped up on the bed. He inched his way toward the black bag. Just as he was about to reach it, he looked up and let out a surprised, "Oh!"

It was Howie's and my turn to put our paws up on the edge of the bed. Looking where Chester's eyes were riveted, we saw a plate sitting on the night table on the other side of the bed. The plate was filled with limp, white lettuce.

"Déjà vu," said Chester.

"I'm fine, thank you," I replied. "But, Chester, this is really no time to practice your French."

"'Déjà vu' is an expression used when something seems familiar, Harold, as if what is happening now has happened before."

"Oh. Well. I knew that. And I'm still fine, thanks. Although I am getting hungry." I was hoping that Mr. Monroe was still planning on making pancakes.

"I see what's happened here," Chester said. "The Monroes left a plate of salad on the night table—remember, Miles had asked for salad *without dressing* to be placed by his bed for a midnight snack. Was that the reason he wanted it there, or was it to lure Bunnicula out of his cage—into a fiendish trap?"

I thought Chester might be onto something. After all, that limp, white lettuce sure looked like Bunnicula's handiwork.

"But where do you think Bunnicula is now?" I asked.

Chester's eyes strayed back to the bag on the bed.

Howie gasped. "We've got to free him!" he yipped. "We've got to let the cat out of the bag!"

"Bunnicula is a rabbit," I pointed out.

"Yeah, but who ever heard of letting the rabbit out of the bag?"

By now Chester was struggling to get the bag open. "It's stuck," he mumbled. "Umph! Come on, you two, give me some teeth."

I can't say I love the taste of leather, but the thought that Bunnicula might be trapped inside gave me no choice but to hop up on the bed and join Chester and Howie in the rescue operation.

It was inevitable, of course, that at the moment the three of us were gnawing away at Miles Tanner's prized possession he would appear in the doorway and cry out, "Stop!"

We jumped off the bed and raced down the stairs faster than you could say "steel-plated Crypto-fleas."

"Now he'll *never* want to use me as a character in one of his books," Howie whimpered as we skidded to a halt on the kitchen linoleum. There before us were the Monroes, wearing coats pulled on over their nightclothes. They were all staring at the same thing.

It was, in Chester's words, déjà vu all over again. For there, in the center of the kitchen table, was a mound of white vegetables: carrots and zucchinis and tomatoes and string beans.

"Bunnicula was here," I whispered to Chester. "That's good, right? At least we know he's not in the bag."

"Perhaps," said Chester, "but then where is he?"

"And where's Edgar?" I asked.

"That's easy," said Chester. "Edgar went off to meet with the head crow. Why do you think Miles opened the window?"

"Ah, yes, the head crow."

"I'm ready!" a voice called out behind us.

We turned to see Miles Tanner, towering over us in his black cape and a mood to match.

"Upstairs I saw . . ." he began.

"We are in *so* much trouble," Howie muttered.

" . . . the window . . . open. That must be how . . . Edgar . . . got out."

Chester snorted. "As if he didn't know," he said. "Oh, it's all theater, I tell you."

"I'm sorry," Mrs. Monroe said. "We forgot to tell you there was no screen on that window."

"Do you think Bunnicula got out that way, too?" Toby asked. "If he jumped . . ."

"No," Mr. Monroe said, squelching Toby's

fear. "Look at these vegetables. He must have managed to get down the stairs and into the kitchen and—"

"Through the pet door!" said Pete, pointing.

"Right!" Mr. Monroe cried. "Let's go!" He waved a flashlight and threw open the door. We rushed into the yard, and what we saw there brought us to a standstill.

There were crows everywhere. On the grass. In the trees. In the air. Other than the occasional flapping of wings, they didn't make a sound.

"Omens," Chester hissed.

I didn't try to talk him out of it this time. Omenwise, a swarm of silent crows in a backyard is in a whole other league from a raisin in a bowl of oatmeal.

Suddenly a single bird cawed loudly. We looked up and saw it sitting on a branch, its mouth opening as it continued to caw. Next to it on the branch perched another crow, this one making a bobbing motion, bowing up and down, up and down. And then it stopped, looked directly at us, and swooped in our direction.

"It's Edgar!" Miles shouted.

At the sound of his name, Edgar flew toward us . . .

and then flew off . . . and then back to us, and then away.

"He's beckoning us," Mr. Monroe said. You have to love a man who can use the word "beckoning" in a sentence before he's even had breakfast. "He wants us to follow him."

And so we did.

SEVEN

Astonished in the Pumpkin Patch

It didn't take long for us to figure out where Edgar was leading us. For there, in the garden behind the last house on our block, was a blur of black and white caught in the beam of Mr. Monroe's flashlight.

"It's Bunnicula!" Toby shouted.

"But what's he doing in Amber's garden?"

"It's Delilah's garden, too," Howie said with a wistful sigh.

Amber, as you may remember, is rumored to be Pete's girlfriend. Delilah is Amber's new puppy. Howie and I met Delilah on a recent jaunt around the neighborhood. After a perfunctory hello to me,

Delilah joined Howie in an interminable round of—not to mince words—sniffing. I will spare you the details; suffice it to say that I have spent much of my life trying to rise above this barbaric canine greeting ritual. In any event, the sniffing routine was followed by an equally interminable game of nip-and-chase. In the end, it was clear that Howie was as smitten with Delilah as Pete is with Amber.

But I digress. It was not Delilah or Amber or any other member of the Gorbish family that was the reason Edgar had brought us here. It was Bunnicula—and something more. Bunnicula had disappeared behind a pumpkin. But was it an ordinary pumpkin? Oh, no. This pumpkin was white!

"How . . . astonishing," Miles remarked as we approached. "I've never seen a white pumpkin. Which reminds me. When I went upstairs to get my . . . cape . . . I noticed that the . . . salad next to my bed had turned . . ."

"White," said Mr. Monroe.

"Yes, how did you know?"

"Vegetables in the kitchen turned white, too," said Mrs. Monroe, "although how in the world he got them out of the refrigerator I can't imagine."

"He?" asked Miles. "Surely you don't mean . . ."

"It's Bunnicula," said Pete. "He's turned vegetables white before, like I told you in my letter. But I sure never saw him turn a *pumpkin* white! That's—"

"Astonishing," Miles repeated, licking his lips. His eyes glowed. His face had more color.

Edgar flew to him, landing on his shoulder.

"Did you bring me here to see this?" Miles asked.

Edgar nipped his ear.

"Astonishing," Miles said for the third time in a matter of minutes.

Now it so happens that there *is* such a thing as a white pumpkin. I know this because I saw it on public television. Chester isn't the only one who learns a thing or two now and again, although I confess that technically this wasn't research on my part. This was Mr. Monroe sitting down to watch a program and my refusing to get off the couch.

In any event, it was quite clear—as Mr. Monroe was now explaining to Miles—that this was not the kind of pumpkin that was *meant* to be white. For one thing, all the other pumpkins around it were orange. For another, this one wasn't *entirely* white. If you looked carefully, you could see a hint of orange. And finally, there were two tiny marks on it, marks that would be easy to miss if you didn't live in a house with a rabbit who was fond of getting his nutrients by sinking his fangs into vegetables and draining them of their juices.

When Miles bent down to look at the marks, he said, "Astonishing."

He is a man of few words. Or in this case: one word.

We had become so distracted by all this talk about pumpkins, however, that we had forgotten about the culprit who had turned this one white.

"There he goes!" Pete called out. "We've got to catch him!"

There he was indeed, and off we went in pursuit of our runaway bunny. Edgar was in the lead, of course, but with his long legs Miles came in a close second.

As we were running home, it began to grow light.

"Bunnicula must sleep soon," Chester said, panting alongside me.

"I can't take this kind of workout first thing in the morning," I complained. "It's too early, my joints ache, I'm old, and I'm lazy. And what do you mean, Bunnicula must sleep soon?"

"He's a vampire, Uncle Harold," Howie piped up. "He can't let the sun's rays touch him or . . . oh, it's too terrible to say!"

"He's . . . rounding the corner of your . . . house!" we heard Miles cry out just before he himself rounded the same corner.

By the time we caught up with him, Miles was shaking his head. "We lost him," he said. "I'm . . . sorry."

"He can't be far," said Mr. Monroe. "He always goes to sleep just before daylight. Odd habit, that. I've never understood it. But at least we don't have to worry about him for now. Let's go in and have breakfast. We'll search for him again later."

"Promise?" Toby asked plaintively.

"Of course, son," said Mr. Monroe. "I'm sure he's sleeping soundly under a bush or under the house. We'll find him."

Needless to say, Chester had his own thoughts on the subject.

"I don't think it's any mystery where Bunnicula is," Chester told Howie and me when we were out on the front porch for a post-breakfast bath and nap. I'm pleased to report that I scored *two* strips of bacon, a mere one hundred and twelve shy of what I feel certain I could digest without tummy troubles. "Clearly it's all a pretense, an act, a charade, a sham . . ."

"Chester," I yawned, "have you been at the thesaurus again? We get your point. Sort of. Well, actually, not at all."

"Fine. Then try to stay awake, Harold, and I'll explain. Obviously, Miles and Edgar—partners in crime—have Bunnicula stashed away in their room."

"How is that obvious?" I asked. "We saw Bunnicula on the loose."

"We did indeed, Harold. We saw him on the loose *until* we didn't see him anymore. And when did we stop seeing him?"

"This is impossible to follow," I said. "Could you make the questions multiple choice?"

Chester ignored me and went on. "We stopped seeing him after Miles and Edgar went around the corner of the house. I feel certain that he's in the guest room in that black bag, undoubtedly in an especially deep sleep because of all the vegetable juices he's imbibed."

"But Pop," said Howie, "what about the pumpkin and the vegetables in the kitchen?"

"And seeing him before we stopped seeing him," I put in.

"Oh, he got out. They were counting on that. But

then Miles caught him, don't you understand? He caught him, and hid him under his cape, and took him back up to his room."

"But why? Why would they do it?" My head was starting to hurt.

"They have plans for him, Harold. They wanted to see if he was as unusual as Pete's letter made him out to be. That's why Miles asked for *undressed* salad to be available at all times and for Bunnicula to be placed in his room."

Howie began giggling.

"What is so funny?" Chester asked.

"Undressed salad," Howie said, and the giggling got louder.

Chester heaved a sigh, shook his head, and continued. "Bunnicula, enticed by the lettuce on the night table, got out of his cage, drained the greens, and then—his unnatural appetite whetted—slipped out the door to go down to the kitchen and from there to the garden down the street. Edgar followed him—undoubtedly with the help of the head crow and the gang of varmints in the backyard— and then returned to wait for Miles. And now they have him in that black bag, right where they want him, and what they're going to do with him is anybody's guess. But I'll tell you this: Whatever else is in that bag—it's not meant for anything good."

It all sounded a little crazy, but then I thought back to everything that had happened. And I began to wonder: Were we really harboring a madman—and a no-good crow—under our roof? Was Bunnicula in danger of being transformed into some kind of steel-plated monster? And would I ever have a conversation with Chester that didn't end up giving me a headache?

It was too much to think about. I did the only thing a dog could do under the circumstances. I closed my eyes and fell fast asleep.

EIGHT

Too Late?

I managed to get about two-thirds of my normal morning naptime in before the tapping started.

"Chester," I mumbled, "get off my eyeballs."

"Then wake up, Harold. This is urgent."

Recalling our last conversation and thinking that Bunnicula might indeed be in the black bag in the guest room, I forced my eyes open.

"People are going to arrive soon, Harold. We have to act fast. Toby and Mrs. Monroe are out looking for Bunnicula, not that they're going to find him. And Mr. Monroe is in the kitchen making lunch."

"Does he need help?" I asked, suddenly wide

awake. "Is that what's urgent?" There was the smell of pot roast in the air. The *urgent* smell of pot roast.

"No, he does not need help," Chester said emphatically. "Now pay attention. Pete's up in his room doing who knows what, and Howie's in there doing who knows what with him. The point is, the coast was finally clear, so I stationed myself outside the guest room, and you will not believe what I heard! Bunnicula's in danger, Harold. Real and immediate danger."

The hairs began to rise along my back. "What makes you think so?"

"I heard Miles say to Edgar, 'He doesn't have to *remain* a rabbit. I could turn him into a bat, like the others.' The *others*, Harold! There have been others before Bunnicula! And then he said, 'Yes, I'll do it!' And *then* he said, 'Edgar, what would I do without you?'"

"So Edgar really is his right-hand bird," I commented.

Chester narrowed his eyes and nodded knowingly. "I told you that crow was no good."

"But he hasn't said 'nevermore,'" I pointed out.

"When he gets his voice back, he will, Harold.

But we've got to stop him before he does. We've got to stop them both!"

"But how? What can we do?"

"We have to break into the room. Right away, before it's too late. Follow me."

I gulped. We could get into serious trouble, breaking into the guest room. But I was convinced we had no choice.

As we climbed the stairs I was haunted by several thoughts:

1. *Bunnicula might already have been turned into a bat.*
2. *I, too, might be turned into a bat.*
3. *That pot roast sure smells good.*

When we got to the guest room door, it was wide open. Chester and I poked our heads in.

95

"There's no one here," I observed.

"No one except Bunnicula," Chester said.

"Bunnicula? Where? I don't see him."

Chester nodded in the direction of the black bag sitting on the bed. "I'll try to set him free, while you stand guard," he said. "Hopefully, the transformation hasn't already taken place."

I have to admit I was rather touched by Chester's new protectiveness toward Bunnicula. For years he had tried to destroy the bunny, believing he was a vampire. But then, after saving Bunnicula from a near-death experience, Chester changed his tune. He still thinks Bunnicula is a vampire, but he has become his friend and protector. "After all," he reasons, "Bunnicula only attacks vegetables. What's the harm in that?"

I cannot tell you how many times in the past I had said those very same words to Chester. But Chester has to come to things in his own time, in his own way, before he'll believe them to be true.

"Are you standing guard?" he asked.

"Standing guard," I replied as he jumped up on the bed.

My eyes and ears were open to the prospect of Miles's or Edgar's return from wherever they'd gone. But it was not my eyes or ears that tipped me off to trouble. It was my nose. Being a dog, I have a finely tuned sense of smell, and I admit that it was fully engaged with the pleasurable scent of pot roast wafting up from the kitchen. So fully engaged, in fact, that at first I didn't notice the other odor coming from the opposite direction. When I did smell it, it set off an alarm in my brain at once.

"Chester!" I cried. "We may be too late!"

Chester looked up abruptly from where he was hunched over Miles's black bag. "What do you mean?" he asked. "I've almost got this clasp open!"

"But I don't think Bunnicula is in there," I told him. "I think he's in another room, being transformed into a bat this very minute! Can't you smell it?"

Chester lifted his nose and sniffed the air. "You're right!" he gasped. "That *does* smell like a bunny being transformed into a bat!"

He jumped down from the bed and cried, "Let's go!"

We charged down the hall and came to an abrupt halt in front of Pete's bedroom. My eyes filled with tears, but whether that was because of the incredible stench emanating from the other side of the door or the thought of what was happening to Bunnicula, I couldn't be sure. All I knew was that there was a very good chance we were too late. We *had* to get inside.

I began pawing at the door as Chester meowed for all he was worth.

Howie yipped from the other side.

Pete called out, "Go away!"

I couldn't believe it. Miles had turned his two biggest fans into unwitting accomplices. How had he done it? Had he convinced them that this was nothing more than a magic trick, easily undone, when the truth was that Bunnicula would be transformed into a bat forever?!

I pawed harder and, despite my distaste for it, began to bark.

Mr. Monroe called up the stairs, "Pete! What's going on up there? Your mother and Toby aren't back yet, and someone's knocking at the door. Would you please answer it? My hands are covered with flour. What is that smell? And Harold, why are you barking? Pete, do you hear me?"

Pete's bedroom door flew open. "I hear you, I hear you!" he shouted as he flew past us and down the stairs.

Chester and I looked inside his room and gasped at what we saw. There, with his back to us, was Miles Tanner, hunched over Pete's desk. As usual, Edgar sat on his shoulder. And on the bed behind them lay a bat, its wings spread open.

Chester saw it at the same time I did and came to the same sorrowful conclusion.

"Dead," he pronounced solemnly. "The experiment was a failure."

"Oh, Bunnicula," I moaned. "We *were* too late."

"We've got to show Mr. Monroe," Chester said. "Grab him, Harold."

"Grab who?" I asked. "Miles? Edgar?"

"Bunnicula, of course!"

"But . . . he's a bat. A dead bat."

"I'm aware of that. Now just grab him and run to the kitchen. Maybe there's still life in him. Maybe Mr. Monroe can call the vet. Maybe . . . maybe . . ."

I saw the look of desperation in Chester's eyes. What was the point of telling him how hopeless it was?

I ran to Pete's bed and grabbed the bat that was once Bunnicula.

Edgar flew at us, flapping his wings and snapping his beak. Miles jumped up, knocking over whatever it was that was on Pete's desk.

"Oh!" he exclaimed. "You startled us! And now look at this mess!"

I ran out of the room, Bunnicula tight in my

jaws, and headed toward the stairs, where I collided with Pete and Kyle, who were on their way up.

"Where are you going?" Pete asked. "Hey!"

"Hey," said Kyle, "why does Harold have your old rubber bat in his mouth? Am I too late for the experiment? Did you get the volcano to work? I can't believe you got M. T. Graves to help you with your science homework! That is so cool. What's that smell? Is that the volcano? It's not what we're having for lunch, is it? It's gross. How come your cat is always washing his tail? You have really weird pets. Hey, do you think Mr. Tanner would want to meet *my* pets? They're not as weird as yours, but . . ."

Kyle's voice trailed off as the boys disappeared into Pete's room, and I spat out the rubber bat and looked for Chester. He was sitting as far down the hall as possible. I don't think I need to tell you what he was doing.

"That must be the cleanest tail in town," I remarked.

He took his time answering. "A slight misjudgment. A wee misinterpretation of the data. Not that I blame you, Harold."

"Blame *me*?" I cried. "But you're the one who—"

"Harold, Harold," Chester said. "Let's not play the blame game, shall we? The important thing is that the transformation has not taken place. Yet. We can still stop it in time. What we need is a plan."

"Oh, no," I said with a shudder. "Not another plan." Chester's plans have a way of—how shall I put this?—not working out.

There was a knock on the front door.

"Coming!" Mr. Monroe shouted from the kitchen. "Pete, Kyle, Miles, our guests are starting to arrive! I hope your mother and Toby get back soon! Pete, please come down here!"

"Just a minute, Dad!" Pete called back. "We're cleaning up! The animals messed up our experiment!"

"I've *got* it!" Chester said. "But we must act quickly!"

"Chester, does this involve any more rubber animals? Because I've got to tell you, the taste of latex lingers."

Chester snorted. "No rubber animals," he said. "Now here's the plan." And he whispered it in my ear.

"You want me to do *what*?" I blurted when Chester was through telling me.

"Sshh!"

"But . . . but that could hurt Bunnicula. It could *kill* him! I thought this was about saving him!"

"Don't worry," Chester said. "He's sound asleep. He'll be so relaxed he won't feel a thing. Now, go quickly, before Miles notices."

Did you ever find yourself doing something that, even while you're doing it, you're asking yourself, "How did I get myself into this? Have I lost my mind?" Well, this was one of those moments. Of course, I have a lot of those moments, living with Chester. But this was one of the craziest ever. There I was, hiding in the closet in the guest bedroom, clutching Miles Tanner's precious black bag in my teeth, waiting for a signal from Chester to make a mad dash and . . . oh, I couldn't bring myself to think about the last part.

"Bunnicula," I whispered, "if you're in there, please forgive me for what I'm about to do."

I heard the sound of footsteps as Miles and Pete and Kyle passed quickly by the open guest room door and down the stairs. I heard the flapping of Edgar's wings. I heard the front door open and a woman's voice saying, "Hello, I hope we're not early." I heard the timer go off in the kitchen. I heard Mr. Monroe call out, "Pete, please make our guests comfortable. I'll be right there!"

And then I heard Chester say, "This is it, Harold. Go!"

NINE

The Truth About Edgar and Miles

My heart was racing as I burst out of the closet, dashed to the top of the stairs, and with a snap of my head flung the bag into the air and on its way to the entrance hall below! Watching it bounce down the steps, I could only pray that Bunnicula would remain asleep inside, so that he would be limp and not get hurt. Seeing the bag that was heading straight toward her, Ms. Pickles screamed as some other woman I didn't know jumped back, twisted her heel, and fell into the arms of the man behind her. Catching her, the man dropped a tray of cookies, which landed with a clatter. The noise made Howie howl, which made Mr. Monroe run into the room, which made Howie run *out* of the room, which made Mr. Monroe trip over Howie, which made the platter of crackers and cheese he was carrying go flying. The black bag landed with a thud at the bottom of the stairs, spewing its contents out into the room. I strained to see if Bunnicula was safe, but all I could make out were peoples' legs going wild trying not to step on cookies or crackers or cheese or whatever *had* spilled out of the bag. Miles covered his ashen face and shouted, "*Nooo!*" as Edgar took off from his shoulder and began circling the house, opening and closing his beak in soundless frenzy. As if they could hear him, the crows in the yards began to screech a discordant chorus, and at that moment . . .

The front door opened and Mrs. Monroe and Toby entered. Toby was carrying something in his arms. Even from the top of the stairs I could see what—or should I say *who*—it was. There, blissfully asleep, was Bunnicula.

"Chester," I said as calmly as I could manage under the circumstances, "got a moment? I think we need to have a little chat."

"We thtill don't know what wath in the bag," Chester replied.

I didn't even have to turn to know that he was bathing his tail.

As for the bag, all was about to be revealed—if not understood.

"What in the world is going—" Mrs. Monroe started to say, when Edgar made what appeared to be a nosedive for Bunnicula. Toby yelped, turned away, and clutched the bunny to him, forcing Edgar to change direction and fly out the open door.

"Come back!" Miles cried as the crows outside cheered Edgar's escape.

Kyle ran to the door and closed it. "Don't anybody panic," he said. "If we go into the basement, the birds can't get us. Mr. Monroe, did you find any plywood yet for the windows? I'll help you put it up. I know how to use a hammer. I've been using a hammer since I was five. Remember that time I had that swollen thumb? Well, I can use a hammer better than that now. Boy, this is exciting! It's like being right *inside* one of your books, Mr. Tanner!"

Ms. Pickles said, "I should say it is! I've been talking to students for years about books coming to life in their minds. I had no idea they could come to life in their very own houses!"

Everyone began to laugh then—everyone but

Miles Tanner, that is. He was staring in horror at what lay on the floor at his feet.

Pete was looking, too. "Are these *yours*, Mr. Tanner?" he asked.

Miles lifted his gaze to Pete's eyes. He opened his mouth, but nothing came out. After a few seconds of shocked silence, he ran up the stairs, sending Chester and me into a tailspin as he whizzed past. The guest room door slammed shut with a resounding *bang!*

Chester and I made our way quickly down the stairs to see what all the fuss was about. Everyone was looking down at the mess on the floor now: the cheese and crackers, the cookies and trays . . . and the contents of the black bag. I could hardly believe what I saw.

The floor was covered with stuffed animals.

Pete was the first one to speak. "You guys," he said to Kyle and Toby between clenched teeth, "if either of you tells anybody at school that M. T. Graves travels with a bag full of stuffed animals—"

"Why would we do that?" Kyle interrupted. "Hey, I used to have stuffed animals."

"I still do," Toby piped up.

"Okay, admittedly it's a little weird for an old guy

to have stuffed animals," Kyle went on, "but what's the big deal, right? To each his own, right? Besides, we have bigger worries right now. Those birds are sounding pretty mean. We'd better get some plywood and—"

Ms. Pickles laid her hand gently on Kyle's shoulder. "I don't think we need to be worried about the crows," she told him.

"No?"

"No, but we may need to be worried about Mr. Tanner."

"I agree," said the man, who turned out to be Pete's teacher. "I think he was embarrassed that we all saw this."

The other woman knelt down and started putting the stuffed animals back in the black bag. "Peter," she said, "I think you're the one to talk to him."

"Me?" Pete squeaked. "Why me?"

"You're the contest winner," the woman said. "You're the reason Mr. Tanner is here."

"And you're the principal," said Pete. "So I guess I'd better do what you say, huh, Ms. Kipper?"

Ms. Kipper smiled. "I'm off duty, Peter. I'm not telling you what to do, just what I think."

Mrs. Monroe took the sleeping rabbit out of

Toby's arms and handed him to Pete. "Take Bunnicula up, knock on the door, and ask Mr. Tanner if you can put him back in his cage."

"Where was he, anyway?" Pete asked.

"Sleeping under the porch," said Toby.

I could hear Chester muttering something about having made "a teensy little glitch in the logic department" as Pete tucked Bunnicula in one arm, grabbed the bag of stuffed animals with his other hand, and started up the stairs.

He was about halfway up when Miles appeared at the top.

"Forgive me," Miles said in his soft, gravelly voice. "It was . . . rude of . . . me to run . . . away like that. Rude and . . . cowardly."

"It's okay, Mr. Tanner," said Pete. "I was just coming up to—"

"No, I will come . . . down," Miles said. "We will . . . talk."

And so it was that we gathered in the living room to learn the truth about Edgar and Miles.

After settling himself into the corner of the sofa, Miles looked around the room and let out an enormous sigh. Just as he was about to speak, Ms. Pickles sat down next to him.

"It's all right," she told him in a reassuring voice. "You're among friends."

Chester perked up his ears at that. "Interesting," he muttered to me. "Sounds like we're about to hear a—"

"You may wonder why I asked to stay here with you," Miles began. "Normally, I would stay in a . . . hotel. Well, there really is no 'normally,' since I never visit schools. I never go . . . anywhere. But you would think I would want to stay in a hotel. You would think so, except that . . . I wanted to meet your pets, you see, because . . . I wanted . . . Bunnicula . . ."

"Confession!" Chester hissed in my ear. "Here it comes! I was right, after all!"

Miles cleared his throat and glanced nervously about the room. "I was hoping, you see, that . . . Bunnicula . . . might . . . inspire me."

Pete said, "But I thought Edgar was your . . . um, what's that word again, Mr. Brooks?"

"Muse," said the English teacher.

"Ah, my muse, yes," Miles said. "He is that. My muse and my companion. My world, really."

"But what about your other pets?" Toby asked.

"Yeah, what about the wolves and bats and alligators and—"

Miles held out his hands to stop Kyle from going on. "There are no other pets."

The room fell silent. "The wolves, the bats, the castle on the mountaintop, the sorcery—all of them are as invented, as imaginary as M. T. Graves himself. All in the interest of making the author of the FleshCrawlers series creepy at best . . . and interesting at the very least."

"But you said you got your ideas from your life," Toby chimed in. "So your life must be pretty interesting, right?"

"I write scary books because I'm scared," Miles admitted. "That's how my ideas come from my life."

"But you write the scariest books *ever*," Pete said. The color was rising in his cheeks. "I don't understand. What could *you* be scared of?"

Miles turned to Ms. Pickles, who nodded and smiled at him in a "go ahead, you can do it" sort of way. I had the feeling these two may have talked more than we knew when Ms. Pickles had dropped off the pretzel crust Jell-O mold.

"I'm scared of . . . dogs, for one thing," Miles began.

Howie gasped.

"And cats . . ."

Chester purred.

"And people. I'm scared of going to the school tomorrow. I'm scared of . . . everything."

"Are you scared of Bunnicula?" Pete asked. He was still cradling the sleeping rabbit in his arms.

Miles looked fondly at the bunny. "No, I'm not. I guess that's because I never had a rabbit . . . bark at me."

This made everybody laugh, even Miles himself. But then he grew serious again. "You see, I've always been so . . . scary looking, so . . . ugly, even as a boy, that dogs barked at me, cats hissed at me, other children laughed at me. So I learned to keep to myself. A writer's life was the perfect life for me. I could have my revenge on the animals that tormented me by transforming them into things even uglier and scarier than I ever was. And I could be alone."

Ms. Pickles started to object, but Miles put his hand on her arm to stop her. I noticed that she let him keep it there.

"But then my books became popular and there were requests for me to speak and visit schools. I didn't dare, even though at times I thought the loneliness would kill me. Then Edgar came into my life and . . . everything changed. I didn't want to transform the animals in my stories anymore. I wanted to stop being afraid of animals in real life. I wanted to stop being afraid, period. I thought perhaps if I could get to know other animals . . . and replace Edgar with . . . someone else . . ."

"Why do you have to *replace* Edgar?" Pete asked.

"Marjorie . . . er, Ms. Pickles . . . was right. He's a wild animal. He doesn't belong in a cage or even a house, which is only a bigger cage, after all."

"But hasn't Edgar always been with you? Wouldn't he miss you if you set him free?"

"I believe he would miss me. I *know* I would miss him. But, no, he hasn't always been with me. It was a stormy night almost two years ago, a very windy night, when I heard a thump at my front door. I opened it, and there on my doorstep lay a wounded baby crow. I couldn't believe it. The image of a crow—Edgar Allan Crow—had been part of the FleshCrawlers series from the beginning, but there never was a real Edgar Allan Crow—until now. I nursed him back to health, and he stayed on with me. We became devoted friends. Edgar was, as you say, my muse. I stopped feeling lonely and I began to write with renewed vigor.

"But then one day a large murder of crows appeared in the yard, and I saw a yearning in Edgar I'd never seen before. He wanted to be with his own kind. I was afraid I would lose him—especially after the time he succeeded in escaping. I saw him fly to another crow and I understood that . . ."

"Aha!" said Chester. "The head crow! Now we're going to get the confession!"

"Edgar had fallen in love."

"Or not," said Chester.

"He's courting," Ms. Pickles interjected. "That's the bowing we've seen him to do with the female crow."

Miles's ashen face turned slightly pink. Was I imagining it, or was he blushing?

"Fearing that Edgar would leave me, I began to have trouble writing. I truly believed I couldn't do it without Edgar. And my confidence wasn't helped by the fact that since a certain boy wizard came along, my sales have plummeted like Niagara Falls. Hoping to improve sales and get me writing again, my publisher came up with the idea of this contest.

"When I read Pete's letter, I thought I had my answer. I would stay in a house with dogs and cats to overcome my fear, and I would spend time with a most unusual rabbit in the hopes that he would inspire me. He has done that, and even more. In a very short time, I have grown quite fond of him. And so now I must ask something . . . difficult . . . for me . . . to ask. . . ."

Just then, we were startled by a loud tapping on the window behind the sofa. There, peering in at us, was Edgar Allan Crow.

"Yes, yes," Miles said, turning to look at him, "I was just getting to it."

Edgar opened his mouth soundlessly, and Miles turned back. He looked around the room, finally bringing his eyes to rest on Pete and the black-and-white bundle in Pete's arms.

"Peter," said Miles, "I know this is a great deal to ask of you and your family. But may I . . . might I . . . *have* Bunnicula?"

TEN

Farewell

I could hardly believe my ears! Miles Tanner was asking to take Bunnicula away with him—forever! He wanted *our bunny* to be his new muse and companion. I turned to Chester, who sat dumbfounded, his tongue half out of his mouth, his eyes as glazed as an Easter ham. The whole room had come to a standstill, all except for Howie, who began bouncing around on his back legs and yipping his head off.

"Take me! Take me!" he yipped. "I'm a better muse than Bunnicula! I'm cuter than Bunnicula! I stay awake more than Bunnicula! Sort of. Take me!"

Miles shrank bank into the sofa cushions as Mr. Monroe got Howie to stop his noise.

"I'm sorry," Mr. Monroe said to Miles.

"No, it's not Howie's fault. I guess I still have some work to do on that," Miles said. "My therapist— Dr. Verrückt Katz—said I should start with stuffed animals and work my way up to the real things."

"You know Howie isn't barking at you because he thinks you're ugly or scary," said Mrs. Monroe. "He's excited. I think he likes you."

"And you're not ugly or scary at all," said Marjorie. "On the contrary. As for stuffed animals . . ." She opened her purse and took out a tiny stuffed lion. "I call him C. L.," she said. "It stands for 'Cowardly Lion.' I take him with me everywhere, for courage."

"Wait right here!" Pete shouted. He stood up and thrust Bunnicula into Miles's arms before racing up the stairs and back down again in a flash. He held a stuffed koala bear.

"This is Pudgykins," he told Miles. "I've had him since I was real little. Now I keep him under the bed in case . . . well, in case I need him, I guess." He shot a look at Kyle and Toby that said, *If you ever tell anybody about this, you are dead meat!*

Miles smiled. "Thank you," he said. "Thank you

for being so kind. I know I'm asking too much of you. I had never intended on asking it. I just wanted to be around Bunnicula, to see if he inspired me. And I was inspired! I began writing a new book last night—even if I did end up turning the rabbit character into a bat. But I got frightened and thought I couldn't do it without Edgar. And then I realized that Edgar had something else in mind entirely."

"Edgar?" said Mr. Monroe.

"Yes. You see, I couldn't understand how it happened that Bunnicula was placed in my room, and why you put a salad next to my bed. And then I

discovered an e-mail addressed to you that I had never written. It had to have been written by someone else, and there was only one other 'someone else' that could have done it."

"Edgar," Mr. Monroe repeated.

Miles nodded. "Edgar is mute. He has never spoken, never uttered a sound. I suspect it's because of his injury when he was young. But being a crow, and therefore a remarkably clever and adaptive creature, he taught himself how to write by watching me. It was he who wrote that e-mail to you, to ensure that I would spend a good deal of time with Bunnicula and get to see him in action. He wanted Bunnicula to be his replacement. You see, Edgar could have left me long ago, but he doesn't want me to be alone. He is the most considerate of birds, the gentlest of souls."

"Ah!" I said, turning to Chester. "So *that's* what 'nefarious' means!"

"This is no time for jokes," Chester snarled. "We're about to lose Bunnicula, can't you see? If they let Tanner take him away from us . . ."

Were my eyes deceiving me? Was that a tear rolling down Chester's nose?

"Yes," Pete said. "You can have him."

The rest of the Monroe family started to object,

but they stopped when they saw the look of hope on Miles's face.

"Really?" he asked.

Chester began to sniffle next to me.

And then I thought I heard Howie barking. I cringed at the sound. But when I saw everyone in the room staring at me, I realized it wasn't Howie who was barking. It was me. Me, who hates the sound of it. I was barking and Chester was sniffling and the humans didn't seem to have a clue what to do about any of it.

Were we really going to have to say farewell to our bunny?

"You know, Miles," Ms. Pickles said then, patting him on the arm, "there may be other ways to solve this. I don't think the Monroes really want to part with their dear pet. And I don't think you'd really want to have them do so."

"*I* have a rabbit for you, Mr. Tanner!" shouted Kyle. "See, one time Pete and I did this hare-raising project for Scouts. That probably sounded like a joke, but I didn't mean it that way. I mean we bred rabbits. And Bunnicula was the dad, and I have his son, see—Sonnicula! And the other day my mom said she was afraid she was developing an allergy to him and maybe we should find him a new home. And so what if he goes to live with you?"

Miles looked down at the sleeping rabbit in his arms. "It wouldn't be Bunnicula," he said.

"No," said Kyle.

"But it would be fine."

Everyone cheered. And Chester began to purr.

The next day, after Miles returned from visiting Pete's school, we all went out into the backyard to say farewell to Edgar. Ms. Pickles was there and so was Kyle. And so was Sonnicula, although—since it was still daylight outside—he was sound asleep on Miles's bed up in the guest room. Miles took to Sonnicula right away, although he said—and who would argue—that no one could ever really replace Edgar.

Now we watched Edgar's flock flapping its wings in anticipation of leaving. Suddenly one of the birds flew down and landed on Miles's shoulder. He nipped him on the ear, and Miles stroked his feathers.

"You've been a good friend," Miles said. "Thank you for everything. I will never forget you. Never."

Edgar flew off to join the one who was waiting for him. And then he flew back one last time, grabbing Ms. Pickles's scarf in his beak and drawing her toward Miles. He hopped onto Miles's shoulder and tugged at his ear until Miles was forced to move toward Ms. Pickles. Once their arms were touching, he flew down to grab the cuff of Miles's shirt, pulling it up until Miles's hand was in Ms. Pickles's.

Miles turned red and smiled at Ms. Pickles.

"Clever bird," he said.

Miles and Ms. Pickles lifted their eyes skyward as Edgar flew off, and the birds rustled and flapped and began to grow smaller in the distance.

"Goodbye, Edgar!" Miles called. There was a catch in his voice as he cried out, "Will you forget me?"

The crows spread out across the sky and went into a formation, and the formation was a word, and the word was:

A Letter Within a Letter Within a Final Word from the Editor

I am writing this from my sheep farm in northern Vermont. My yard is filled with crows, and I find I have grown quite fond of these birds, with their shiny feathers, saw-toothed cries, and mischievous ways. I like to imagine that Edgar and his family may be among them, but then I also find myself searching pumpkin patches for white pumpkins with a hint of orange.

I can't help being a bit sentimental when I think how fortunate I was to be able to edit this book. For it helped me see that change is a good thing, even if it means letting go of what's safe and known. As Harold has always said, "Life is an adventure, and adventures are meant to be shared." So here I am, sharing my adventures as a sheep farmer with my family and looking forward to whatever life has in store for me.

Not that I'm done with editing entirely, mind you. My publisher asked me to continue working on a handful of books from my farm. And there's a certain young writer whose books I look forward to editing. But I'll let Harold explain. I received the following letter from him a short time ago:

My dear friend,

I hope you are doing well. All is well here in the Monroe household. We are relieved that Bunnicula is still with us—even Chester, who maintains that that was not *a tear and he did* not *sniffle at the thought of Bunnicula being taken from us. He claims he was having an allergic reaction. To what, he never said. Still, I can't help but notice that he is more protective of Bunnicula than ever and spends an inordinate amount of time around his cage.*

As for me, I am enjoying my retirement from

writing, although I must admit I will miss visiting you in your office. I was especially fond of the snack machine at the end of the corridor. However, should you ever need help with your sheep, I would be happy to pay a visit (I do have some herder in me), and I know Howie would love to come along if you have any crows that need chasing.

Pete received a letter from Miles the other day, and I thought you would enjoy knowing what he had to say:

I have good news! Marjorie and I are to be wed! I will be moving to Centerville, because I do not want her to have to leave your school library, where she feels so at home and needed. So we shall be neighbors!

(Do I have to tell you that Howie practically did cartwheels on hearing this news?)

The other good news is that I am writing again. My brief visit with you motivated me to write _two_ books! The first, which I have just completed, is entitled <u>Quoth the Raven</u>. It is the story of my relationship with Edgar, and I am publishing it under my own name: Miles Tanner. "M. T. Graves" will continue to write the Flesh-Crawlers books, although no animals will be transformed or harmed in any way in the making of those books—ever again. Instead of the story about the rabbit (that turned into a bat), I've written an entirely different book called <u>The Excellently Weird Adventures of Charlie the Cat from Galaxy Nine!</u> Can you guess who inspired that one?

Needless to say, Chester is less than thrilled that he is to be a "psycho-creature in one of M. T. Graves's demented novels." But Howie is beside himself that we will all be characters in the final scene of Quoth the Raven, which takes place in our own backyard at the time Edgar is set free.

Encouraged by the visit from his favorite

*author, Howie has begun writing his own
books. I think they might turn out to be rather
good. May I send you the first one when he's
finished? It has something to do with a mad scientist and a stuffed animal named Pudgykins. I
think you will like it.*

I think I *will* like it. I'll miss working with
Harold, but it's always good to work with beginning writers. Everyone needs a change. Everyone
needs something new. Everyone needs good company and the inspiration it brings.

And now I must go tend my sheep.

HAROLD MONROE is the nom de plume of Harold X, dog by day, writer by night (and sometimes by day, when he isn't napping). Harold has written other books about his family and their adventures: *Bunnicula, Howliday Inn, The Celery Stalks at Midnight, Nighty-Nightmare, Return to Howliday Inn*, and *Bunnicula Strikes Again!* He is also the author of *Why Is My Food Dish Empty?* a mystery thriller that remains unpublished. He did not plan on becoming a writer, but years ago when an unusual rabbit joined the household and vegetables mysteriously started turning white, *someone* had to write about it—and it certainly wasn't going to be Chester, who was too busy hyperventilating and saying things like, "Today vegetables, tomorrow the world!"

Harold loves chocolate, especially chocolate cupcakes with cream in the middle. He is also fond of broccoli, bacon, and banana cream pie, although not together. Now that Howie is writing books, Harold is looking forward to retiring. He plans to spend his golden years enjoying his hobbies, which are eating, sleeping, and . . . well, eating and sleeping.

Despite the fame and fortune his books have brought him, Harold does not own a cell phone.

HOWIE MONROE is the nom de plume of Howie X, even though he really has no idea what a nom de plume is and thinks X is a weird last name. The talented, smart, funny, clever, and cute-as-a-button wirehaired dachshund puppy has been writing books since twelve thirty. Just kidding. He's been writing books ever since M. T. Graves came to stay at his house and his uncle Harold found an unused notebook under Pete's bed. In a burst of creative genius, he wrote six books, and they've all been published! The series is called Tales from the House of Bunnicula, although Bunnicula isn't in any of them. That was his publisher's idea. If he'd had his way, the series would have been called Tales from the Talented, Smart, Funny, Clever, and Cute-as-a-Button Mind of Howie Monroe.

Howie's first book, *It Came from Beneath the Bed!*, is about a mad scientist (Pete Monroe) and a koala bear named Pudgykins. It's pretty good, but Howie thinks his later books are even better, even if none of them has ever won a Newbony Award. He thinks *Screaming Mummies of the Pharaoh's Tomb II* (which he wrote with his friend Delilah) not only should have won a Newbony Award, it should have been made into a movie—and maybe a TV series. None of which has happened.

Life is unfair. Especially if you're a writer. And a dog.

When he isn't writing, Howie Monroe likes to chase birds, bark at Joe the mailman, and make hysterically funny jokes.

Howie wants to thank M. T. Graves for inspiring him, Uncle Harold for helping him, and readers everywhere for reading him.

Look for Howie's Tales from the House of Bunnicula series wherever fine books are sold—or under your bed, because you never know what you'll find there.